PRISONER'S FRIEND

Robert Ashe, a cheerful-looking man approaching forty, is a prison visitor, popular with the warders. The youngest and most promising of his prisoners, Terry Booth, is almost due for discharge, and Ashe possibly has a job for him in a garage. He meets the owner of the garage, Laurence Winter, and his charming, but somewhat coy wife, Mavis, who both seem happy to give Terry a chance at 'going straight'. Terry has a violent past but Ashe is almost sure he can be trusted. That is, until it is discovered that someone has attempted to steal some cash from the garage office, and then a dreadful murder is committed—and Terry has disappeared...

PRISONER'S FRIEND

Andrew Garve

· BLACK ·
DAGGER
· CRIME ·

First published 1962
by
Wm. Collins Sons & Co. Ltd.
This edition 1997 by Chivers Press
published by arrangement with
the author

ISBN 0 7451 8703 X

British Library Cataloguing in Publication Data available

Printed and bound in Great Britain by
Redwood Books, Trowbridge, Wiltshire

FOREWORD

PRISONER'S FRIEND is a fast moving thriller which exemplifies
Andrew Garve's talent as a storyteller. The basic premise is
simple. Robert Ashe, a middle class prison visitor, helps Terry
Booth, a young man with a violent past, to start a new life on
leaving jail. Ashe helps Terry to find a job working at a garage
owned by Laurence Winter, but soon has cause to worry about
whether Terry is really going straight. When murder occurs
and Terry flees, it seems as though Ashe's good intentions
have had a disastrous outcome. But although the
circumstantial evidence against Terry is strong, the police are
unable to charge him even when they finally track him down.
Ashe puzzles over the mystery and comes to realise that the
truth about the case is both grim and unexpected; his problem
then is to convince those in authority he is right.

Garve's simple, fluent style of writing is crucial to the book's
success. There is no shortage of twists and turns in the plot and
the pace with which events unfold impels one to keep turning
the pages. One reviewer likened his work to that of the once
celebrated Freeman Wills Crofts, but in truth the comparison
does Garve no favours; his literary skills are far superior to
those of Crofts. Garve's gift for economic yet effective
characterisation is worth noting, as is his restraint: he does not
make the mistake of crowding his stories with too many
people or an excess of incident. As often in his books, the hero
is not a professional detective, but an ordinary man whose
determination to see justice done enables him to overcome a
series of seemingly insuperable obstacles. Ashe is a likeable
fellow, a veterinary surgeon who is not without faults,
including a mild but human tendency to boastfulness. He even
has his own equivalent of Sherlock Holmes' Dr. Watson in his
level-headed wife, Nancy. The policeman heading the official

murder enquiry, Inspector Mayo, is by contrast a minor character, although not a shadowy one. Garve neatly contrasts Mayo's views on penology with those of Ashe, but although it is clear where Garve's sympathies lie, he is never didactic.

Garve's novels are admirably varied, and he is equally at home with adventure, espionage or detection, but a recurrent element is sailing. In *Prisoner's Friend* too, activity on a small boat plays a central part in the puzzle. Ashe strongly suspects that the murder was the end product of an ingenious conspiracy. The seasoned reader will not be altogether surprised that a complicated scheme is ultimately unravelled; what is so appealing about the book is the way in which Ashe battles on when the odds seem stacked against him.

Prisoner's Friend was written in the days when murder was still a capital crime and the atmosphere of the period (the immediate pre-Beatles era) is well conveyed. Sadly, it is almost 20 years since Garve's final novel, *Counterstroke*, was published. Yet his craftsmanship is such that his work can still be read with much pleasure. No doubt his writing skills derive from his long experience as a journalist; under his real name, Paul Winterton, he was once on the staff of *The Economist* and later worked as reporter, leader writer and foreign correspondent for *The News Chronicle*. His books include *A Student In Russia* (published in 1931, when he was 23) *Eye-Witness On The Soviet War Front* and *Mending Minds: The Truth About Our Mental Hospitals*, but after 1948 he concentrated on fiction. He was a founder member of the Crime Writers' Association and, with Elizabeth Ferrars, its first joint honorary secretary. Although he wrote crime novels featuring series characters under other psuedonyms (Roger Bax and Paul Somers), it is the Garve books which have best stood the test of time. *The Megstone Plot*, another clever conspiracy thriller, was one that was successfully filmed and, although it is not quite in the same league, *Prisoner's Friend* is another vivid story that might well have transferred most effectively to either the small or large screen.

MARTIN EDWARDS

Martin Edwards is the author of five novels about the solicitor and amateur detective Harry Devlin. The first, *All the Lonely People*, was short listed for the Crime Writers' Association's John Creasey Memorial Award for best first crime novel of 1991. It has been followed by *Suspicious Minds*, *I Remember You*, *Yesterday's Papers* and *Eve of Destruction*. The Harry Devlin novels and short stories have recently been optioned for television.

THE BLACK DAGGER CRIME SERIES

The Black Dagger Crime series is a result of a joint effort between Chivers Press and a sub-committee of the Crime Writers' Association, consisting of Marian Babson, Peter Chambers, Peter Lovesey and Sarah J. Mason. It is designed to select outstanding examples of every type of detective story, so that enthusiasts will have the opportunity to read once more classics that have been scarce for years, while at the same time introducing them to a new generation who have not previously had the chance to enjoy them.

PRISONER'S FRIEND

I

THE CLOCK in the tower was just striking six as Robert Ashe swept into the forecourt of the prison and pulled up with a jerk before the castellated gatehouse. He was a large, brown-faced, cheerful-looking man, approaching forty, with bright periwinkle eyes and a great Roman beak of a nose. He knocked out his pipe, tossed his hat into the back of the car with a slightly extravagant gesture, strode purposefully across to the prison entrance, and pressed the bell.

There was the sound of a distant footfall and, after a moment, of rattling keys. Then the small wicket gate opened, and the gatekeeper looked out. " Ah—Mr. Ashe," he said. " 'Evening." He glanced up at the clear May sky. " A nice one, too, by the looks of it."

" Better out than in, eh, Thomas? " Ashe said with a grin, as the wicket gate clanged behind him. He took the shining key the officer gave him and secured the chain to his clothing. Then he was passed through the iron grille that formed the opposite end of the gatehouse, and was in the prison proper.

He went first to the Visitors' Room to collect his book. He no longer needed to refer to it for the names and cell locations, the offences and sentences of the six prisoners on his visiting list, but he wanted to see if anything had been done about a suggestion he'd made the previous week that someone should call on Fogarty's wife and try to clear up a domestic compli-

5

cation. He turned up the entry and saw that the
governor had written beside it, " Noted. Will be
arranged." Satisfied, he recrossed the prison yard and
rang for admission to the hall where all six of his men
had their cells. Again he received a friendly greeting
from the officer who let him in. The prison warders
liked Ashe—perhaps because he so clearly had a good
opinion of them. Their job, he'd come to realise, de-
manded an exceptional combination of virtues—
courage, tact, a sense of humour, unwearying patience,
and restraint. The last two qualities seemed to Ashe
particularly admirable because by nature he didn't
have them.

From the ground the hall looked rather like the hold
of some great ship, with the sky visible only through
lights from the deck far above. On each side rose tier
upon tier of iron doors, each separated from the next
by a few feet of painted brickwork. The upper stories
were approached by steel and concrete landings which
overhung the central passageway and ran its entire
length. Between the landings there were steel ladders
which ascended from the centre of the hall and zig-
zagged up into the roof.

Ashe had been visiting the prison now for nearly two
years, but he was still affected by the place each time
he saw it—by its feeling of inexorable strength and
hardness, its uncanny quiet, its scrubbed, antiseptic
smell; by the worn treads and handrails of the ladders,
polished by countless generations of prisoners, and the
great wire net spread at first-floor level to deter any
would-be suicides. Sentiment, he knew, was out of
place in the job he'd undertaken, but it was impossible not to feel compassion for men caged like beasts.

Especially when, as in Ashe's case, life outside seemed so exhilarating, so full of zest and interest. Some people said that prison to-day wasn't a sufficient deterrent to crime. All he knew was that it would have deterred him!

He began to mount one of the ladders, fingering his key. At first it had seemed strange and incongruous to him that he should be allowed to move around in the hall, unaccompanied and unwatched, with a key at his waist that would unlock any cell. Indeed, he had found himself toying fancifully with the notion that if he had a mind to he could let everyone out— and he'd imagined, not without pleasure, the headlines in the newspapers afterwards—PRISON VISITOR FREES THREE HUNDRED. SAYS " DID IT ON IMPULSE ! " To-day, however, he had no such off-beat thoughts—his mind was firmly on his job. He climbed quickly to the top gallery and went straight to D.5.24, the cell of Terry Booth, the youngest and most promising of the prisoners on his list. Usually he took the six cells in order as they came, even though he often spent more time with Terry than with the others—but to-day his first concern was with the young man, who was almost due for discharge. He reached the cell, unlocked the door, fixed it behind him so that it couldn't slam shut but still gave privacy, and went in.

The cell was long, high, and narrow. Its walls were of limewashed brick above a coloured dado. The floor was of stone. Opposite the door was a window, of small panes fixed in a steel sash, with a sliding panel to let the air in. · There was a plank bed and coir mattress, a table and chair, a washstand, and a couple of shelves. Terry was sprawled on the bed in trousers and singlet, reading an illustrated paper. It was a sign of the special interest the authorities had in him that, in this chronically overcrowded jail, he had been given a cell to himself. There was to be no risk of last-minute contamination.

He got up as the door opened. He was a powerfully-built youth of twenty-three with a pear-shaped head, thick, curly hair springing from a widow's peak, and an obstinate mouth and chin. His eyes had a look of wary intelligence. He would have been reasonably prepossessing if his face had been less battered. His nose had taken heavy punishment at some time, and there was a scar along his right cheekbone where some-one had slashed him in a street fight.

At the sight of his visitor his features relaxed in a welcoming grin, which much improved him. " Hullo, Mr. Ashe," he said.

Ashe said " Hi!" and gave him a brief, friendly handclasp. After more than forty weekly visits, repre-senting some twenty solid hours of increasingly un-inhibited talk about almost everything under the sun, his relationship with Terry had no trace of formality or self-consciousness or awkwardness—no false notes. It wouldn't, in any case, have been in Ashe's nature to be patronising or condescending. He had many faults, but those weren't among them. He had no self-im-portance, no side, no snobbery, almost no class sense, no use for cant or sham. What he had was a struggling honesty, and a secret awareness of inadequacies in himself that was half-way to understanding the failures of others. It was that—more than anything, perhaps —that had made him such an acceptable prison visitor. With Terry, in particular, he could chat almost as easily in the cell as though they were meeting for a pint in a pub.

He sat down on the edge of the table, his favourite perch. Terry sat on the bed. Usually at this point they'd have started to exchange their bits of news—Ashe talking about his job, perhaps, or the antics of his young family, Terry recounting some prison incident, something about the work he'd been doing during the week. There'd have been talk about motor racing and Grand Prix drivers—one of Terry's enthusiasms, but a subject that Ashe had had to mug up like algebra. There'd have been argument and raised voices and banter and undoubtedly—when Ashe got warmed up—laughter. Argument and laughter went with him everywhere—loud, robust laughter, as often as not at himself. To start with, as a greenhorn visitor, he'd wondered about those hoots of mirth, rolling out of the cell into the echoing hall. But he'd been encouraged by authority, not reproached. A bit of frivolity was fine, if it helped to lift the prisoner out of himself. Cheerful visitors were a blessing. . . .

To-day, though, there was nothing of that. Time was short, and Ashe got straight down to business. The business of getting Terry back into society as a useful citizen.

" I had a phone call from the Discharged Prisoners' Aid Society this morning," he said. " It seems there's a man named Winter with a garage in Sussex who's got a place for a young fitter—and he's offered to take an ex-prisoner. Sounds right up your street."

Terry nodded. " I'll say. . . ."

" I've arranged to see him to-morrow—his place is only about seven miles from where I live. But I thought

I'd better sound you out before I talked to him. About whether you'd like it."

" 'Course I'd like to work in a garage," Terry said. He had the cockney glottal stop—but only slightly.

" I know that—but this would be a country job. The garage is on a main road, but there aren't any towns near it. It's in deep country—even the villages are tiny. . . . And you'd be living in the country. Fields instead of pavements, not much to do after work, forty minutes on a bus to the pictures, everything very quiet. Not at all what you've been used to—and my wife says you'd be lonely. Do you think you could stand it? "

" I reckon I could stand anything arter this lousy dump," Terry said. " Any rate, I wouldn't 'ave to stay, would I?—not if I didn't like it. . . . So what's the bloomin' worry? "

Ashe shook his head. " You'd have to make up your mind to stick it for a bit, Terry. That's why I want you to be sure. It wouldn't do you any good to start chopping and changing jobs right at the beginning. . . . So just think about it for a minute."

Terry appeared to think. " Okay," he said, with a faint shrug. " I guess I'd stick it."

" I'd be around, of course," Ashe said. " We'd be able to meet. It would be convenient from that point of view. You'd be able to come and see the family if you felt like it. And I'm sure you'd soon get to know people—country folk aren't nearly as standoffish as they used to be. . . . The thing is, you can't really afford to be too choosy at this stage."

" I'm not choosy," Terry said. " Who's saying

anything? A job's a job, ain't it? I'd take it like a
shot."

Ashe looked relieved.

" All right, then," he said, " I'll see what I can do
to-morrow with Mr. Winter."

" Does he know what I been in for? "

" No. . . . As far as I know, your name hasn't been
mentioned yet."

" When he does, I reckon he'll turn me down."

" He might," Ashe said. " It certainly wouldn't do
to bank on it. But I hope he won't."

Terry sat silent for a moment. Then he said, " I can
tell you one thing, Mr. Ashe—if I do get the job, like,
I won't let you down. You can count on that."

" I should bloody well think so," Ashe said cheer-
fully. " What's more," he added with a grin, " I shall
expect my car to be kept in tip-top order."

" Sure," Terry said, " we'll have it at Silverstone in
no time. . . . What did you say it was? "

" A Ford Consul—1955."

" Cor!—you've got a perishin' hope."

For a few minutes they talked about cars. Then Ashe
looked at his watch and got up. " Well, I think I'd
better be pushing along—we'll have plenty of time for
nattering when you're out. . . . I'll see you get word
about the job, one way or the other."

" Thanks, Mr. Ashe. . . . I hope it's okay."

" And I'll be looking in next week as usual—the last
visit, eh? So long, Terry. Keep your chin up."

" You bet."

Ashe let himself out, locking the cell door behind him.
On the landing he paused for a moment. Fogarty
next, perhaps, to relieve the old fellow's mind about

his wife—and then Mason, the most recent addition.
Now what was the name of Mason's daughter? Oh,
yes—Deirdre. And she was just getting over chicken-
pox. . . . Ashe smiled to himself. It had taken prison
visiting to teach him not to do all the talking, to be
a good listener as well. A useful discipline, no doubt.
But chicken-pox—what a topic! Oh, well. . . . He
walked briskly to the ladder and descended to the next
gallery.

Ashe was a veterinary surgeon by profession and
practised from his home on the outskirts of Springfield
village near the Kent-Sussex border. The house was
late Victorian and ugly, but suitable for the job,
having plenty of space for Ashe's surgery and waiting-
room and study, as well as for the family, and some
outbuildings for the temporary accommodation of
ailing pets. A couple of acres of scrubby, neglected
meadow at the back provided a useful exercise ground.
The practice produced an adequate living, but no
more, and the house reflected this. There was comfort,
but no luxury. Ashe had no assistant, and his wife,
Nancy, no resident maid. A woman came in from the
village to clean each morning, but Nancy did the
cooking and looked after their two daughters—Margaret, aged eight, and Jane, who was nearly five. As
she also kept the accounts of the practice and sent out
the bills, Ashe being a slapdash hand with figures, she
was usually pretty busy.

There were no messages on the hall table when Ashe
got in that evening and he went straight into the
sitting-room, where a modest cold supper was laid out
and Nancy was snatching a few minutes with the paper.

A Siamese kitten dozed peacefully on the arm of a chair. Ashe tickled its ear with a pipe-cleaner as he passed and at once it threw out a paw and scratched him. " Ingrate ! " he said. " How I hate animals ! " Nancy smiled, and he went and kissed her for no particular reason.

Nancy Ashe was seven years younger than her husband and a contrast to him in almost every way. She had none of his flamboyance or extravagance of manner. In appearance she was slim and dark, with a small, piquant face. Where he was temperamental and erratic, she was calm and reliable. Where he was ebullient, impetuous, and often over-sanguine, she was controlled, cautious, and full of common sense, thus providing a much-needed stabilising influence in the family. She had learned to counter her husband's tendency to wild exaggeration with a teasing, fond scepticism, and when he was unreasonable—as he frequently was—she would let his moods break over her like waves on a rock and pass on without damage. She argued with him, when she had to, without heat, and held her own without apparent effort. She knew him well—probably better than he knew her. She thought him quite impossible, she admired him for many things, and she was completely devoted to him. As for Ashe, he leaned heavily on her all the time.

About his voluntary prison visiting, Nancy had rather mixed feelings. She was glad for his sake that he'd found an absorbing interest in addition to his work. As he'd said when he'd taken it up, a man couldn't really be expected to make animals the *whole* of his life. She wished she could have shared his experiences more completely, but by the nature of things she could rarely meet the prisoners herself. At the same time, they were constantly being brought vividly to life for her by Ashe's racy accounts of his visits, so that up to a point she felt that she knew them too. She had serious reservations only about Terry Booth. He was the one prisoner so far whom Ashe had shown a deep personal interest in. Recently the word " Terry " had been heard a great deal about the house, and Nancy was aware of a slight if unreasonable jealousy.

" Well," she asked, as he dropped into a chair, " how did it go? "

Ashe gave a big, eloquent sniff. " That new chap Mason's going to be a pain in the neck," he said. " He was in his despairing mood to-night—couldn't see any use in making an effort. . . . Sat on his bed, sobbing like a kid—said he'd ruined his family and himself and that his life was over. . . . Can I have some beer? "

Nancy poured him a glass. " All quite true, up to a point, I would have thought. . . . What did you do? "

" Oh, I trotted out all the old clichés—while there's life there's hope—fellow who falls and picks himself up is worth more than one who's never tempted. . . . Tried to stiffen him up a bit—appealed to his dignity and manhood. . . . So help me, I even quoted a couple of lines of Kipling's ' If '! " Ashe gave a sudden hoot of laughter at the recollection. " I felt pretty daft doing it, I can tell you—I'm glad no one was listening. . . . Anyway, he calmed down in the end. . . . *I* don't know . . ." Ashe took off his thick-rimmed glasses and rubbed his eyes, massaging the tiredness away.

" Well, darling, if he calmed down you must have said just the right things."

" I suppose so—he *said* I'd done him good. . . . Trevor's being troublesome, too. He told me he'd had a divine revelation during the night—said he'd been converted. Kept walking up and down with his bible, quoting bits at me. . . ." Forgetting his tiredness, Ashe got up too, to illustrate. " He's a fat, unctuous old devil. . . . ' I've seen the light, Mr. Ashe, I'm a changed man.' " Ashe's mimicry was perfect, his mobile, actor's face the very image of an unctuous old devil.

Nancy smiled. " What did you say? "

" I said, ' Well, you'd better see the chaplain about it, Bunyan, because I don't believe a word of it. . . .' Now there's a real rogue for you. . . ."

" *Did* you say ' Bunyan '? "

Ashe grinned. " Well, I would have done—I only just thought of it. . . ."

" And what about Terry? "

" Terry? " Ashe's tone became offhand. " Oh, he'll take the job if it's offered to him—he says he's not a bit worried about the quiet life. . . . I think it would be a good thing—at least it would keep him away from his old London pals. . . . He'll have much less chance of getting into trouble again in the country."

" I wouldn't be too sure about that," Nancy said. She looked thoughtful. " I'll certainly be interested to meet him, though—having heard so much about him. . . . Let's hope the garage man doesn't get cold feet, that's all."

" He won't," Ashe said confidently. " I'll shower him with thanks from the start and then he won't have the nerve to draw back. You'll see—I'll talk him into it."

He caught the look in Nancy's eye—the look she

always gave him when he started to boast. " Well anyway," he said a bit sheepishly, " I'll have a damn' good bash."

The appointment with the garage owner had been made for eleven o'clock to allow time for Ashe to get through his surgery, which was held daily from nine till ten. Always an early riser, he was up particularly early next morning, eager for the day. Before the family had stirred he had removed a splint from a Scottie's leg, neutered a kitten, and fed and tended all the miscellaneous beasts and birds that had been left in his care.

By and large, Ashe enjoyed his work. He was a good vet—an excellent diagnostician and a skilful surgeon—and whatever he might say to the contrary he liked animals. He was proud of his modern surgery, with its up-to-date equipment on which he'd spent much more capital than he could afford, and proud of the diploma that hung on the wall there. It was very revealing that Ashe—a most untidy and careless man in the house, spilling his tobacco all over the place, leaving his clothes on chairs or on the floor, never knowing where anything was—always kept his surgery spotlessly clean and in apple-pie order.

The trouble with the job, as Ashe saw it, was not the animals but the people. The farmers were all right, of course—the bread-and-butter side of the job. They were down-to-earth chaps with livings to earn, and when they asked for help they really needed it. But the pet owners, who in this wealthy district could provide or withhold the jam, were another matter entirely. Ashe didn't mind the genuine eccentrics, for whom he had a fellow-feeling—like Mrs. Creedy, an elderly breeder of bull terriers, who had smoked a pipe for forty years and with whom he could discuss tobacco brands on equal terms. He had nothing but sympathy for people in real distress and would go to any lengths —even absurd lengths—to help them. Once, when a tearful small girl had arrived on the doorstep with a moribund goldfish in a bowl, he had driven straight into Laybridge and bought another of the same size and shade and substituted it and told her it would be all right now! What irritated him were fussy, foolish women with time on their hands who expected him to take a serious interest in their trivial, manufactured anxieties just because they could afford to pay. He also disliked, in his prejudiced way, animal lovers who hunted—there were lots of those around Springfield— and people who left three or four dogs locked up in a car while they went shopping, and people who lavished affection on pets but seemed to hate humans. He had his little list—his mental list—and with these people he was apt to be brusque. The result, naturally, was that his clientele failed to grow as it might have done. Nancy often urged him to use a little more tact and diplomacy, but he couldn't bring himself to—not for long, anyway. He knew the technique, of course. He had it at his fingertips, if he'd cared to use it. For short periods, after Nancy had talked seriously to him, she'd hear him on the job, tongue in cheek, overdoing it, winking at her—ringing up some wealthy client with the latest situation report, in what he called his cage-side manner. " Ah, good morning, Lady Blanke, how are you? Lovely day, isn't it? I've got *very* encouraging news about your budgie, I'm glad to say. He took a good look at himself in his mirror this morning—and he rang his bell twice. I think we're about over the hump. . . ." But it never lasted. " Silly old hag ! " he'd explode, slamming down the receiver. " It'd serve her right if her blasted bird dropped dead ! " And the next client would find him short-tempered, unfeeling. . . .

To-day, however, his mood was excellent. The surgery proved to be a light one, the three callers all pleasant people whom he liked. Two dogs and a cat needed specific treatment for real ailments. . . . He made up ointment, wrapped up phials, shook hands warmly. " Such a nice man—Mr. Ashe ! " By ten he was out of his smock, washed and changed, and on his way in good heart to get Terry a job.

In the course of his rounds, Ashe had often passed what he now knew to be Winter's garage, though he'd never had occasion to call there before. It was a flourishing-looking place at a junction of roads called Scripps Cross, near the village of Shedley. It had an impressive line of petrol pumps in a wide forecourt, with a glass-sided kiosk where the girl attendant sat when she wasn't serving ; a show window with a couple of new models in it ; a row of quite presentable second-hand cars standing outside with their prices limewashed on the windscreens ; and—judging by the signs of activity inside—a busy repair department.

As Ashe drew up away from the pumps, a man came out of the garage and approached him. " Mr. Ashe ? " he said, in a pleasant voice. " How do you do?—I'm Laurence Winter." He was a big man of about Ashe's own age, with a chubby, amiable face. " Let's go into the office, shall we?—it's comparatively quiet there."

He took Ashe through into a smart, well-furnished room and drew up a chair for him. " I hope you haven't been brought too much out of your way. . . ."

" Not at all," Ashe said.

" By country standards I suppose we could almost call ourselves neighbours. . . . Cigarette? " Winter produced a box and gave Ashe a light. " Well, now . . ."

Ashe was making a rapid mental readjustment. He'd expected, though he scarcely knew why, a less sophisticated, more working type of garage owner—a simpler man, who might respond quickly to a breezy appeal. With Winter, the approach would have to be on a rather different level. Ashe's manner became serious and responsible, his speech precise, like Winter's, not slangy as it usually was. He could be quite a chameleon when it suited him.

" I should tell you at once," he said, " that we're immensely grateful to you for your offer of help. It was most kind of you to think of it."

" Oh, I'm afraid I can't take any credit for the idea," Winter said. " I happened to see a programme on television—one of those documentaries they do so well —about the plight of ex-prisoners trying to make a fresh start, and how employers could help. I'd never really thought about it before. . . . It was rather moving, and it left me with the feeling I ought to do something. I employ quite a number of people—I run a small farm as well as this place—and my wife thought it was a good idea. So I got in touch with the aid society that was mentioned in the programme, and they did the rest. . . . Well, now tell me about this young fellow you have in mind."

" His name's Terry Booth," Ashe said. " He's a

single man, aged twenty-four next month. He's keen on everything mechanical, and he's been trained as a fitter in prison. I'm told he's a pretty good one."

" What has he been in prison for? "

" When he was just twenty-one," Ashe said, " he tried to break into a warehouse in London with two other youths. A man who was passing in a car saw them and stopped. Booth dragged him out of his seat and hit him with an iron bar and the three of them drove off in the car. They were chased and caught. The man recovered—though it was a near thing. Booth got three years."

Winter's jaw dropped. " H'm—I don't like the sound of that. . . . It's true I told the society I wouldn't mind a fairly tough youngster, but I didn't mean a thug. . . . Has he been in any other trouble? "

" He hasn't any record," Ashe said. " Officially, this was his first offence. I think he may well have stolen before, but if so he wasn't caught. . . ." Ashe leaned forward earnestly. " I know he doesn't sound much of a proposition, Mr. Winter, but there's his background to consider. This boy never had a chance. . . ."

" Isn't that what they say of most of them these days? "

" In Terry's case I think it's absolutely true. . . . Look, can I tell you something of his history? "

" By all means," Winter said.

" Well, his father was a respectable artisan—but a weak man. His mother was a no-good slut, who cleared off with someone else when Terry was three and hasn't been heard of since. His father divorced her and re-married. The stepmother was viciously cruel to Terry,

especially after she had children of her own. She was
constantly picking on him—he wore out his shoes too
fast, he shut the door too hard—she was always nag-
ging at him. She made it clear she didn't want him.
It was always ' Go away,' ' Get out of my sight.' Often
she threatened him. She'd say things like, ' If you do
that again, you little brat, I'll kill you.' Once she talked
about cutting out part of his brain to make him behave
better—that was when he was nine. His father believed
the lies the stepmother told about him, and beat him.
Terry never had a scrap of affection from anyone—no
kindness, no warm human relationship anywhere. It
was emotional death—and it went on. When his
father died he was farmed out to various people who
didn't care about him either. The result was, he just
came to hate everyone——"

Winter interrupted him. " You got most of this
from Booth himself, of course? "

" Most of it, yes—but, where we have been able to
check, it squares pretty well. I've no doubt it's broadly
true."

" M'm . . . Well, it certainly wasn't much of a start,
I agree."

" I think it explains everything," Ashe said. " With
a background like that, he was almost bound to become a delinquent. He'd been rejected himself, so he
rejected society. He teamed up with a gang so that
he could feel he belonged somewhere. At least there
was loyalty and solidarity there. He led a gang life,
hanging round street corners, rough-housing, boasting
of successes with girls, lounging in coffee bars, plotting
malicious bits of mischief. The usual things. . . . Then
he suddenly planned this warehouse breaking. It

wasn't a rational exploit—there was almost nothing in the place they could have carried away. It was done for the thrill—an act of defiance, of bravado. . . . To give him prestige and status in the gang. As for bashing the man, he'd grown up in a climate of violence—and he'd seen it happen scores of times on the telly. . . . What do people expect? I'm not a trained psychologist, but to me everything that Terry did developed absolutely logically from his background."

Winter nodded slowly. " Yes, it's possible you're right—but even if you are, it hardly solves my problem. . . . Knowing what had made him that way wouldn't be much consolation to me, would it, if he suddenly hit *me* with an iron bar? What I need to know is, has he reformed? Can you vouch for him? "

" I was coming to that," Ashe said. " The truth is, he's changed out of all recognition. When he first went to prison he was hostile and insolent and tough. Everyone was against him, so he was against everyone —that was his line. For a long time he wouldn't have a visitor at all, and when finally he asked for one and I saw him he was completely unco-operative. He swore he'd never reform, he boasted of all sorts of unpleasant exploits—he was brazen and arrogant and contemptuous. . . . What he wanted, of course, was an audience —though I didn't realise it at the time. My reaction was that he was a bumptious lout who badly needed taking down a peg or two—but that was hardly my job and I felt like packing him in. In fact I almost did. It was the assistant governor who persuaded me not to. He said that Terry was a pretty characteristic case, that he was obviously trying to draw attention to himself, to compensate, and that prisoners were often most in need of help when they were at their most unattractive. He recommended patience—and letting Terry talk himself out. So I did just that—I went along, and put up with his talk, and just went on trying to be friendly. And in the end it turned out what he needed was lifting up a peg, not taking down. It was a slow business, gaining his confidence and building him up —but it happened. . . . Now his ugly mood's quite gone—he's a different man. He's co-operative, he's sorry for what he did, and he says he wants to work hard and make something of his life."

" I see. . . ." Winter pondered. " And you think he can be relied on? "

" Personally, I haven't a doubt about it. And all the people who've had anything to do with Terry in prison—the assistant governor, the chaplain, the doctor—agree that he's an excellent prospect."

" But you could all be wrong? " Winter said.

" I don't think we are. . . . Naturally, there's no absolute guarantee—there's always bound to be a slight element of risk. . . . Some prisoners intend to go straight and then backslide through weakness or getting into bad company. Some get crafty in prison and pretend they're going to reform when they're not because they think it will do them a bit of good. I've had a few disappointments—we all have. But I'm convinced that Terry isn't going to be one of them. If I had a job to offer him I'd do it without hesitation."

Winter looked curiously at Ashe. " You feel strongly about him, don't you? "

" I've put a lot into him," Ashe said. " When you've visited a man every week for nearly a year you can't be indifferent to what happens to him after he comes out."

" No, I suppose not. . . . Tell me, what is he like to look at? "

" Oh, he's no beauty—he's been in some bad fights. But that's superficial—I'm sure there's good stuff inside. . . . He's big and strong, he's got quite a lot of personality when you get to know him, he's not unintelligent. . . . He's definitely a cut above most of the corner boys."

" He still doesn't sound to me like everyone's favourite employee! " Winter said.

" Which is exactly why I'm hoping so much that *you'll* take him," Ashe said. " Some ex-prisoners can be placed fairly easily, especially in these days of full employment—but a man with a record like Terry's is a real problem. Naturally, people are scared off. . . . Yet he's just the sort of chap to benefit most from a little timely help. He's young enough to start all over again—young enough to be salvaged. . . . You could be the making of him."

Winter sat silent for a while, thinking it over. Ashe waited, on tenterhooks.

" Well, it's a challenge," Winter said at last, " and I'm inclined to accept the risk. . . . I'll tell you what I'll do—I'll see Booth, and if I don't take a really violent dislike to him I'll give him a trial. . . . How's that? "

" I simply can't thank you enough," Ashe said. He took out a handkerchief and gently dabbed the beads of sweat from his forehead. " I've been pretty worried about him, I can tell you. . . ."

" You're a persuasive man, Mr. Ashe—and, if I

may say so, an eloquent one. You put the case well."

Relieved and relaxed, Ashe grinned. " My wife says I'd talk the hind leg off a donkey. . . . Shocking thing to say to a vet! "

Winter laughed. " Indeed, yes. . . . Well, now, there are still a few things I'd like to know. . . ."

They began to discuss the practical problems of release. Now that he'd reached his decision, Winter seemed most anxious to help in every way he could. He would stamp Booth's insurance card and bring it up to date, he said, and he would advance part of the first week's wage so that Booth would have a little money from the beginning. Naturally, he would pay the normal rate for the job. . . . Ashe beamed at him, as the customary difficulties melted away.

" There's one point I'd like to have clear," Winter said. " Is it going to be generally known that Booth has been in prison, and what he was there for—or will that be between him and me? "

" He doesn't want any secret made of it," Ashe said. " It'll be tougher for him that way to begin with, but I think he's right—if people know all there is to know about him from the start, there'll be nothing for them to discover and make trouble about later. . . . Though, as a matter of fact, I don't imagine it could be kept quiet in this case. He'll have to live somewhere, and I don't see how we could allow him to sleep under anyone's roof with his record of violence without disclosing it. . . . Finding a place for him may prove to be quite a problem."

" Yes, I can see that," Winter said thoughtfully. " I wouldn't feel too easy myself. . . ." He sat frowning.

" You know what we *might* do—I've got a small, empty cottage on the farm that I could put a few sticks of furniture in. Booth could sleep there—and I'm sure my foreman's wife would be willing to have him in for meals, if it was made worth her while. That would largely get over the problem, wouldn't it? "

" It sounds the ideal arrangement," Ashe said.

" Then I'll talk to Mrs. Dyson and see if I can fix it with her. She's a motherly old soul. . . ." He pushed back his chair and smiled. " Well, it's going to be quite an experience, Mr. Ashe, if it comes off. I hope I'll prove equal to it. . . . Is there any advice you can give me about the best way to handle Booth? "

" Only not to think of it as too much of a problem," Ashe said. " The main thing is to treat him naturally —in the same firm, friendly way you would any other employee. Encourage him, of course, praise any good work, try to give him confidence in himself, make him feel he's filling a useful place. Crack a joke with him occasionally. Above all, appear to trust him—even if you don't! "

Winter nodded. " It sounds like good advice—I'll remember. . . . I'll have a word with the garage staff, too—they're decent chaps and I'm sure they'll want to give him a fair chance. . . . Will you be keeping in touch? "

" Oh, yes," Ashe said, " the follow-up is about the most important part of this visiting job. That's when the real headaches start. . . . I'll have my eye on him as long as he needs me."

" Good," Winter said. " I'm glad about that. . . . Well—now I'll have to tell my wife about Booth. . . ." He hesitated. " You wouldn't care to run over and

meet her with me, would you—take a glass of sherry
with us before lunch? We're only a mile from here.
. . . Or are you tied up? "

" I'd very much like to," Ashe said.

Winter looked pleased. " I do think it might be a
good thing if you had a word with her. She was all
for the idea in principle, you see, but she might think
this was going a bit far. . . . I'll just give her a ring and
tell her we're coming."

Ashe couldn't help a slight feeling of envy at sight
of the Winters' home. It was a charming modern
house, built of old, mellow brick, and tile-hung in the
traditional Sussex style. It stood by itself above a
bluebell-covered bank, well back from a quiet lane,
and entirely screened from the road by trees and bushes.
The approach was by a steep, winding drive to the
garage, and then by a flagged path. The lawns around
the house were close-shaven and almost weedless, the
garden beautifully tended and gay with flowers. At
the back there was a paddock of several acres, pleas-
antly dotted with sheep.

" What a lovely place! " Ashe said, gazing around at
the satisfying scene.

Winter nodded. " It is very agreeable, isn't it?
We're lucky to have a really first-class gardener. . . ."
He surveyed his domain appraisingly. "The paddock's
not quite at its best just now—it could do with a lime
dressing. Bit rough at the side, too. . . ."

" It looks all right to me," Ashe said, thinking of
his own tatty field. They started to stroll up the path
towards the house. " How much land do you farm,
Mr. Winter? "

" Oh, very little—no more than forty acres. There used to be a lot more, but most of it was sold off before my time."

" How long have you been here? "

" Just under two years. . . . Dyson—the foreman I mentioned—lives in the old farmhouse and runs the place from there. I give him general instructions, of course, but I'm afraid I'm no more than a hobby farmer—just as I'm a hobby garage owner. I've a manager there, too. I'm not really a very practical chap, but I enjoy dabbling with these things, and as I can afford to—well, I do." He smiled wryly. " It gives me the illusion of being useful."

They were approaching the house now. As they reached the front door, it was opened by a pretty girl of twenty or so, who stood back to let them in. From her demure manner, Ashe judged her to be the maid. Winter said, " Thank you, Sheila," and conducted Ashe into the sitting-room.

A small, elegant woman came forward to greet them, a large boxer dog at her heels. She looked, Ashe thought, considerably older than Winter, but with her excellent figure and smart, well-groomed appearance she was still attractive. Her eyes were blue and bright, her complexion pink. She made Ashe think of a dainty doll, a little worn by time.

Winter introduced them. His wife's name, it appeared, was Mavis. The big boxer sniffed around Ashe for a moment, then nuzzled him with a friendly shove.

" Castor obviously approves of you, Mr. Ashe," Mavis said, in a bright voice. " I hear you're a vet —I suppose all animals like you."

" The intelligent ones do," Ashe said.

" When Castor's not well, which isn't very often, thank goodness, I take him to Mr. Hargreaves. Do you know him? "

" I do indeed," Ashe said. " He and I often stand in for each other. . . . A very good man."

" *I* think so. . . . Well, do sit down. . . . Darling, you might bring that little table over for the sherry. And give Mr. Ashe a cigarette. . . . No, Castor, you can't sit on my feet, you silly boy. . . . So you've arranged about the young man? "

" Yes, it's all fixed," Winter said. " As good as fixed, anyway. . . . You tell her, Ashe. . . ."

Ashe told her about Terry, quite briefly. In spite of her rather butterfly manner, he had the impression of shrewd listening. She looked a bit wide-eyed when she heard what Terry had done, but Ashe quickly re-assured her. " That's all in the past now," he said. " I'm certain there's nothing whatever to worry about."

" Well, I agree he should be given a chance," Mavis said. " After all, he has paid for what he did, hasn't he, and it really isn't fair to go on punishing people for ever. . . ." She smiled. " Anyway, Castor will look after us, won't you, Castor? We're not scared."

Ashe smiled back. In other circumstances Mavis would by now have been well up on his list of animal-doting "tiresomes," but as she was being so helpful about Terry he readily forgave her.

Winter, with a grateful glance at Ashe, passed round the sherry. " Here's to the success of the experiment, then. . . ."

Ashe raised his glass. " To you both," he said.

"And how do you like prison visiting, Mr Ashe?" Mavis asked after a moment.

"Very much," Ashe said. "I find it quite fascinating."

"Do you really? Laurence, dear, could you get us another ashtray, we're both having to stretch. . . . I can see it might be, of course—but some of those men must be so dreadful. . . ."

"Some are pretty awful. Some are very decent—just unlucky. . . ."

"Well, I know I'd hate to go into one of those horrid places myself. . . . I suppose I'm really quite spoiled. . . . Weren't you nervous to start with?"

"I was nervous when I first walked into a cell, yes—I simply couldn't think what to say to the chap. The best thing seemed to be to try and find out something about him, so after a few preliminaries I asked him if he had a wife. He said, 'Yes, sir, *two*—that's the whole bloomin' trouble.'"

Winter guffawed. Mavis smiled. Ashe looked pleased with himself. Actually, the incident hadn't happened to him, it had happened to someone else—but he'd always thought it a good story.

"How often do you go to the prison, Mr. Ashe?" Mavis asked.

"Every week, for an hour or two."

"Good gracious, as often as that?"

"Well, a visitor has to be regular," Ashe said, "that's one of the first things that's impressed on us. . . . If you miss a week, without a very good reason, the prisoners feel let down—feel they don't really matter to you. . . . And that's fatal."

"I suppose so. . . . Well, it's all terribly interesting,

isn't it, Laurence. . . . How do you become a visitor in the first place?"

"Oh, usually someone recommends you—often another visitor. . . . In my case, it was a lawyer client of mine. . . . After that you have an interview, and if you're approved the Prison Commissioners invite you to serve for a year. If you turn out well, they thank you for your services at the end of the year and invite you again. If you don't, they just thank you for your services!"

"That's what would happen to me," Winter said. He was hovering behind Mavis. "A little more sherry, darling?"

"Just half a glass—you know it always makes me so sleepy in the middle of the day. . . . Well, I think it's a terribly kind, public-spirited thing to do, Mr. Ashe."

Ashe shook his head. "It's actually a self-indulgence, Mrs. Winter. Everyone enjoys playing the Good Samaritan, don't you think? The prisoners are so pleased to see you, it flatters your ego. Makes you feel you're important."

"Oh, come, you're underrating yourself," Mavis said.

If she had had a fan, Ashe thought, she would have tapped him with it. Good-hearted, undoubtedly, but a little coy. . . .

He finished his sherry and got to his feet. "Well, I think I'd better be getting along. . . . I'm delighted to have met you, Mrs. Winter, and I'm enormously grateful to you and your husband for giving Terry a chance. . . ."

"We'll do our very best for him," Mavis said.

Outside in the car, Ashe sat for a moment savouring his success. It had been an arduous but triumphant morning. To have got Terry a job at all was an achievement—but to have aroused in his prospective employer a keen personal interest in him was even better. Ashe grinned at himself in the car mirror. " Bloody good, Ashe," he said; " bloody marvellous! " Then he started the engine and drove quickly home to tell Nancy the news.

Ashe's self-congratulation turned out to be a little premature. In all the bonhomie with Laurence Winter and his wife, he'd forgotten that there was still a small hurdle to be overcome—the preliminary interview between Terry and Winter. It took place at the garage a few days later, Terry having been paroled for the purpose. Immediately afterwards, Winter rang up—and to Ashe's consternation he seemed to be having second thoughts. Terry's appearance hadn't at all appealed to him, he said—he'd looked much too much like a young burglar in his Sunday suit! Perhaps, after all, it would be wiser to drop the idea. . . .

Ashe put everything he knew into talking him round again. If Terry was turned down now, he said, it might well have a worse effect on him than if he'd never been offered the interview. Since his own discussion with Winter, he said, he'd encouraged the boy to hope that the job would be his—a statement that wasn't strictly true, since Ashe hadn't seen him, though it seemed a white lie in the circumstances. . . . Terry would be fearfully disappointed, he said—and disappointment could so easily lead to despair. . . . In any case, surely a short trial could do no harm—and

Winter would probably feel very differently about him in a week or two. It was just a question of surviving the first shock. . . .

With a laugh, Winter said that Ashe was a terrible fellow. He certainly didn't *want* to back out—and perhaps it *was* a mistake to attach so much importance to first appearances. . . . Very well, he'd go ahead and give the boy his trial. . . .

There were no more waverings after that, no more hitches. Preparations were started at once for the day of Terry's release. Winter was as good as his promise about equipping the empty cottage for Terry to sleep in, and fixing up with Mrs. Dyson about meals; and Ashe, making his own check, found the arrangements most satisfactory. The cottage was about a mile from the Winters' place, tucked away at the end of an earth track. It was conveniently close to the Dysons, not more than five minutes' walk away, and it wasn't too far from the garage, either. Its two tiny rooms were furnished quite adequately for a single man. Mrs. Dyson proved to be exactly the comfortable, homely type of woman that Winter had described, and very willing to help a lame dog. Ashe told her a bit about Terry, warned her about his battered face so that she wouldn't be too worried when she saw it, and thanked her warmly for what she was doing.

Terry's transition to freedom ten days later, eased by the aid society, went as smoothly as such things ever could. Ashe met him outside the prison gates in the early morning, took him to the cottage, introduced him to Mrs. Dyson, and finally deposited him at the garage for his first day's work. No one, he thought with satisfaction, could have been given a more auspicious start in his new life. Now it was largely up to Terry himself.

During the next few days Ashe was able to catch up with some arrears of work. Nancy, her ear to the ground at the local information exchange, the grocer's, reported that Terry's arrival at Shedley had created a bit of a stir in the district but that most people seemed well disposed towards him. "Give the boy a fair chance," was the general view. Ashe was in touch with Winter by phone from time to time, but he didn't see Terry again until the week-end. Then on the Sunday morning—Terry's first Sunday out of prison and a possibly blank day—he collected him in the car and took him home for a chat and to meet Nancy and the children.

Terry had obviously been at great pains to prepare himself for the visit. He was sprucely dressed in the blue civvy suit he'd been given on leaving the prison, and a clean striped shirt. His hair was carefully brushed, his chin immaculately shaved. In his tough way, Ashe thought, he was far from being an unimpressive young man. Yet it was easy to see what Winter had meant about the dressed-up burglar. With his big muscles rippling under his jacket, and his scarred face, Terry *did* look incongruous—rather like an old-style gangster poshed up and button-holed for the funeral of someone he'd bumped off. Ashe chuckled at the thought. Really, it was most unfair. . . .

"Well, how are you finding the job, Terry?" he asked, as they drove off.

"The job's fine," Terry said.

"Do you like the work?"

" Yes."

" Good. . . . How do you get on with Mr. Winter? "

" He's all right."

" And the other men? "

Terry nodded. " They're decent blokes." He wasn't exactly bursting with enthusiasm, Ashe thought, but then it was hardly to be expected at this stage. And perhaps he was feeling nervous. . . .

" You look as though Mrs. Dyson's been feeding you pretty well," Ashe said.

" Yeah—she's okay. I reckon she likes me all right."

" Are you comfortable at the cottage? "

Terry shrugged. " It's a roof."

" H'm. . . . Tell me, what have you been working on? Anything special? "

" Mr. Winter's car, mostly—it's in for a de-coke. Mercedes—smashing job."

" I thought he had a Rover."

" Yeah, but he's got a Merc too. Boy, that engine! I guess he's pretty rich, eh? "

" I imagine he gets by," Ashe said.

" Go on, he must be stinking. You should see the dough they take at the pumps. . . . Lucky devil! "

Ashe took his pipe out of his mouth—and clamped it firmly back in again. " I'll be bringing this car in to be serviced in a day or two," he said. " Perhaps you'll be doing it."

Terry grinned. " That'll be a treat. . . ."

They were running into Springfield village now. In a moment Ashe turned into the drive. " Well, here we are. . . ."

Terry sat looking up at the house. " Cor—funny old place, ain't it? "

Ashe shrugged—smiling. "It's a roof," he said. "Come and meet the family—I expect they're out on the lawn."

He led the way round to the back. There were two lawns, an upper and a lower, separated by a macro-carpa hedge. The grass was a bit bare, the flower borders a bit unkempt like the field below, but the general effect was pleasant. The children were taking turns on a low swing that Ashe had put up for them. Nancy was watching them from a wide paved terrace under the french window. She turned at the sound of male voices. Ashe presented Terry.

For a split second, as Nancy looked at him, her face went quite blank. Then she smiled. "Hallo, Terry. . . ." She shook hands. "You don't mind me calling you Terry, do you?—I've heard so much about you."

" 'Course not," Terry said.

The children came skipping up. "This is Terry," Nancy said. "Margaret—Jane. . . ." Jane was dark and attractive, like her mother—Margaret had Ashe's nose, fortunately on a reduced scale. The girls shook hands too, eyeing Terry uncertainly.

Jane said, "What's the man done to his face?"

"He fell from a great height," Ashe said. "And if you make personal remarks I'll spank your bottom."

Jane giggled. "Silly old Daddy," she said. She ran back to the swing. In a moment Margaret followed her.

"I'll get some beer," Ashe said.

When he came out again, with an armful of bottles, two glasses, and an opener, Nancy was showing Terry some of the animals in the hutches.

" Perhaps you'd like to see my surgery? " Ashe said.

" You bet! "

" It's one of the best in the south of England. . . ."

Terry grinned. " Yeah—you told me."

" Did I? I suppose I did. . . . Anyway, let's have the beer first." He poured a glass. " Try that. It's made specially for export. . . ."

Terry tried it. " Lovely," he said. He stood in silence for a moment. He seemed to be listening. " Remember what you said abaht the country, Mr. Ashe? Well—you was right."

" Too quiet for you, is it? "

" Quiet! Cor—it's terrible. Sort of noisy quiet— all them ruddy birds in the morning. I'd like to shoot the perishers. . . . Beats me how you stick it."

" It's just a question of what you're used to," Nancy said. " Have you been into Laybridge yet?—it's not so quiet there."

" I been in once. Cost me nearly three bob. . . . I'll 'ave to get meself a push-bike, I reckon."

" That's not a bad idea," Ashe said.

" I begun saving up. . . . What I'd really like's a motor-bike—somethink what really goes."

Ashe smiled. " Brands Hatch, eh? Well, there's nothing like having something to work for. . . ."

On the whole, Ashe thought, as he drove Terry back for his midday meal at the Dysons', the visit had passed off as well as could be expected. Terry had been a bit more laconic than usual, a bit grouchy—he was clearly some way yet from settling down in a contented fashion. But it could only be a question of time before he found his feet, developed some interests, made friends. The important thing was to see that he didn't mope on his own in the meantime. Terry had said he was going to look over a second-hand tractor with Dyson in the afternoon, so he should be all right for the rest of that day. . . .

Nancy was in the kitchen, preparing to dish up lunch, when Ashe got back. He went straight in there. " Well," he said, " what did you think of him? "

Nancy hesitated.

" Of course," Ashe said, " he wasn't at his best this morning. You've got to remember that everything's strange to him—*we're* strange. . . . You've got to make allowances."

" I realise that," Nancy said slowly. " I've tried to remember everything. . . . But I can't honestly say I like him, Robert."

" Why not? "

" Well, he looks so . . . brutal."

" That's only because of the scar on his face—and I warned you about that. You'll soon get used to it. I have."

" I know you have. . . . It isn't only that, though— it's his whole appearance. There's something about his eyes—they're like pebbles. Callous. . . ."

Ashe snorted. " Pure imagination! You're seeing him that way because you happen to know he clobbered a man with an iron bar. If I'd brought him along and introduced him as a promising young vet who'd had the bad luck to be tossed by a bull and flung on his face you'd have liked him at once."

" I'm quite sure I wouldn't," Nancy said, smiling. She went to the window and called the children in. " I may feel differently about him when I get to know him better, I realise that. . . . At the moment, I wouldn't trust him farther than I could see him, that's all."

Ashe was disappointed at Nancy's attitude, but he wasn't entirely surprised. He had sensed for some time her slight jealousy over Terry and he knew she hadn't been keen on his coming to Sussex. . . . Really, she'd been all set *not* to like him—but she'd get over it. There was nothing to be unduly disturbed about. . . .

He was much more dismayed when Laurence Winter's developing view of Terry turned out to be remarkably similar to Nancy's.

" According to my manager, he's a good worker," Winter said, when Ashe looked in at the garage a day or two later. " He's a competent mechanic, he seems anxious to learn, and I've no complaints at all about his behaviour. But somehow I just can't take to him."

Ashe looked worried. " I'm sorry to hear that," he said. " Very sorry."

" I'm not alone, either—my wife feels the same way about him. We had him up one evening—it seemed the decent thing to do when he's so obviously at a loose end after work, and naturally she wanted to see him. . . . I don't know what it is about him, Ashe— there's a sort of wariness, a lack of frankness. I feel all the time that he might be quietly thinking up some mischief."

" Oh, I'm sure he's not doing that," Ashe said. " I know what you mean about the wariness—but that's hardly surprising, is it? I'd say he was finding everything a bit overwhelming. It can't be easy for him, trying to get adjusted. Wondering all the time what people are really thinking of him. . . . Anyone would be on the defensive."

Winter nodded. " Yes, I suppose so. . . ."

" As for lack of frankness, I must say I haven't noticed it. If anything, I find him rather outspoken."

" H'm—I wish he would be with me. He knows you so much better, of course. . . . Ah, well, it's early days yet. . . ."

Nancy still hadn't met the Winters, and at the week-end Ashe suggested she should ring them up and see if they were free for a drink before dinner—which she did. Mavis Winter sounded very pleased and accepted at once for the Sunday evening.

Ashe found it an agreeable occasion. Terry was only briefly referred to. Mavis seemed to take to Nancy at once, and was soon chatting to her as freely as though they'd known each other for weeks. Ashe and Winter, sitting a little apart from the women, found their own topics. Winter, it appeared, was an enthusiastic sailing man and kept a cabin cruiser on an Essex river to which he and Mavis often repaired on fine week-ends. His lively accounts of adventures and misadventures on the water kept Ashe entertained—and Nancy once or twice glanced across with a smile, too, as though she'd caught something interesting. Then Ashe had to show Winter his surgery, and Mavis said she'd like to take a peep at the children. When the party broke up, Winter said it was a shame they hadn't got to know each other earlier, and Mavis said they must all meet again soon.

After they'd gone, Ashe said to Nancy, " You and

Mavis seemed to be in quite a huddle. What was all that she was telling you? "

Nancy made a bit of a face. " Her life history, darling."

" Was it interesting? "

" Not exceptionally. She was telling me about her first husband, who died. Apparently he was quite devoted to her, and she felt frightfully lonely afterwards —she hasn't any children, which is a great sorrow to her. So she travelled round and round the world, and then two years ago she met Laurence and that transformed everything because now *he's* quite devoted to her."

Ashe laughed. " You are a bitch! Didn't you like her? "

" I didn't *dis*like her," Nancy said. " She's quite lively and amusing—though I do think she's a bit self-centred—and rather bossy. . . . We hadn't really very much in common—after all, she isn't even my generation."

" Oh, come off it," Ashe protested, " she's not all that old."

" I'm sure she's well over fifty."

" Then she's worn jolly well, that's all I can say."

" You wouldn't be aware, of course," Nancy said, " but she did have a rather marvellous make-up, and she obviously spends a fortune on her hair. . . . It must be easy to wear well if your husband has oodles of money and you live a completely sheltered life. . . . Did you notice her pearls? And those clothes—I was green with envy. . . . I should think she's a very pampered woman."

Ashe grunted. " If you ask me, you're getting pretty

critical these days. First Terry, and now Mavis! What about Laurence? "

Nancy smiled. " Oh, I like *him*," she said. " I think he's a charmer! "

The next few weeks were a period of marking time as far as Terry was concerned. He was reported to be still working quite well, though in a rather shut-in, cheerless way. Unless there was something special on the Dysons' telly that he wanted to see, he tended to mooch about the lanes a good deal in the evenings, on his own. In general, he had little to say for himself. He wasn't hostile, but he wasn't sociable. Occasionally he went into Laybridge, to the pictures or a pub, but always alone. His mood improved a little, but only a little, when towards the end of June he managed to acquire a very old bicycle, which he repaired and painted himself. He was at least mobile now in his spare time—though he still hadn't anyone to be mobile with. Ashe saw him fairly often, but he was well aware that what he needed was a friend of his own tastes and choosing. In that direction Terry seemed unwilling to make any effort. He repulsed rather surlily an attempt by the local youth club leader to rope him in. He wasn't, he said, going to be shoved around with that bunch of kids. The Winters persevered in having him along to their house in spite of their private misgivings about him—though they weren't sure whether he came because he wanted to or because he'd been invited by his boss. It was all rather difficult. Still, Ashe remained quite optimistic about the future. Terry didn't strike him as having any unexpected or insuperable problems, anything particularly on his mind. When they were together they talked easily and freely, and Terry seemed cheerful enough then. He was probably, Ashe decided, just lonely.

In these weeks, Ashe and Nancy saw quite a lot more of the Winters. Ashe and Winter, brought together in the first place by their common concern for Terry's welfare, had by now found other matters of mutual interest. Some of them were professional— Winter had had trouble with a flock of ewes after an unusually wet spring and was anxious for Ashe to take a look at them and advise him. Ashe, through long association with farmers and their problems, was himself quite knowledgeable about the land, and Winter appeared to enjoy talking to him about his modest farming plans. There was a personal aspect, too. Winter made no secret of his admiration for Ashe— for his energy, his independence of mind, his extrovert, exuberant nature—and did his best to cultivate him. Mavis, for her part, obviously believed that in Nancy she had found the ideal listener. So the acquaintance ripened—a little one-sidedly. Winter was keen that Ashe should spend a sailing week-end on the boat with him, and Ashe said he'd like to—though he didn't quite know when he'd be able to fit it in. Nancy had to side-step several invitations from Mavis. As she said, it was all very well for the Winters, who were people with leisure and almost no responsibilities—but a fairly regular exchange of visits to each other's houses was quite a problem when there were two small children to think about. . . . Ashe fully agreed with her. He liked Winter, and was enormously grateful to him, but he'd decided he didn't care for Mavis any more than Nancy did—and even as things were he never seemed to have enough time for all the things he had to do. Better, he said, not to get too involved. . . .

It wasn't until the middle of July that any real improvement occurred in Terry's outlook on the world —but when it came it was dramatic. Quite suddenly, he was going about looking cheerful and smiling. He was heard whistling at his work. He was seen playing light-heartedly with Mrs. Dyson's children. He was even reported to have told Dyson that the cottage wasn't a bad place for a single chap, and that he was getting used to the country. . . . Ashe didn't press him at once for an explanation of the miracle—he was thankful enough that it had happened.

Terry himself volunteered the explanation a week or so later, over a glass of beer in the local pub. " I got meself a girl friend, Mr. Ashe," he said.

So *that* was it! Ashe was delighted.

" That's really good news, Terry," he said. " I'm so glad. . . . Who is she?—anyone I've met? "

" Yeah, you've met her. It's Sheila—Sheila MacLean, Mr. Winter's maid."

Ashe looked quite taken aback. " *Really?* Why—I didn't know you knew her."

" I didn't till couple of weeks ago," Terry said, with a grin. " But I'd had me eye on her, right from the start—trouble was, we wasn't ever left alone. Then, Sunday before last, she was cleaning her bike when I got there, and I arst her if she'd come out for a ride with me, on the quiet like, and she said she would and she did. She's a real nice chick and she likes me —we get on fine. Understand each other, see? I reckon we'll be going steady."

" H'm . . ." Ashe still hadn't quite adjusted to the news. " You *have* been a dark horse, haven't you? Do the Winters know? "

" Shouldn't think so," Terry said. " Any rate, *we* haven't told 'em. Why should we? It ain't none of their business what Sheila does in her free time."

" Still, I'm sure they'd be interested. . . . Actually, I'd have thought the news would have got around in a place like Shedley."

" Oh, we was careful, see—met on the downs in a place Sheila knew, Saturday afternoon. Didn't want people sticking their noses in. . . . Now it's different—we're fixed up, like. We don't care who knows."

" You must be a very fast worker," Ashe said. He looked thoughtfully at Terry. " Well, this certainly has been a great surprise. . . ."

" Goin' to wish me luck? "

Belatedly, Ashe realised that he hadn't done. " Of course—all the luck in the world. . . . She seems a very nice girl."

" You're dead right she is," Terry said. " Nicest kid I ever come across."

Nancy was aghast at the news.

" The girl must be off her head," she said. " I suppose she feels sorry for him. . . . It's the only possible explanation."

" Go on," Ashe said, " you're biased. . . . He's a big, strong, well-set-up young fellow—I can quite imagine a girl finding him attractive. The right girl. . . . You know—' the mysterious alchemy of love.' "

Nancy's eyebrows went up. "'Mysterious' is the word! I'd be afraid to be alone with him."

"Well, *she* can't be. . . . She's obviously fallen for him in a big way."

"I think it's most dangerous," Nancy said. "He's probably only fooling with her and I'm sure she's very inexperienced."

"We don't know much about her, do we?—we've never seen her for more than a few seconds. . . . I can only just remember what she looks like."

"She looks inexperienced, darling."

Ashe grunted. "The way she'd kept things to herself, she could be pretty deep. . . . Knowing quiet places on the downs! Anyway, I didn't get the impression Terry was fooling."

"He always has been, hasn't he? If half the things he's told you about his goings-on with girls are true, she could be riding a tiger."

"Probably a lot of it was just talk," Ashe said. "Besides, he's changed since then. . . . I'd say he's really fond of her."

"I wonder what the Winters will think about it," Nancy said.

The Winters, when the news reached them, were as taken aback as Ashe had been, and as full of qualms as Nancy. Laurence Winter's normally genial countenance was quite troubled when he talked to Ashe about it later that day.

"Of course," he said, "Terry was bound to find a girl somewhere sooner or later—and it's a good thing he has. . . . But we'd have preferred it hadn't been Sheila. Mavis is extremely annoyed about the whole thing—she says she wishes now we'd never asked him along. Apart from anything else, she feels they've both been rather sly."

" Yes, I'm sorry about that," Ashe said—and paused. " Mind you, young people don't usually shout their affairs from the house-tops, do they? Lovers *are* a bit sly. . . . Especially when they're—h'm—feeling their way, so to speak."

A smile flickered over Winter's face. " Well, that's true enough. Still, there it is—Mavis is very much against it. She talked to Sheila pretty plainly this morning—told her she was taking an enormous risk, and that Terry wasn't to be trusted, and that she'd probably live to regret it if she went on seeing him. . . . Sheila just stood there, deadpan—it didn't seem to have the slightest effect."

Ashe showed no surprise.

" Mavis asked her if she'd told her parents about him, and she said she hadn't, and wasn't going to. They live up in Northumberland—keep some sort of shop. From what I've gathered they're unusually narrow and strait-laced — they belong to some peculiar religious sect. Take sandwiches to a tin chapel every Sunday morning and stay all day, Sheila once told me. Her father's a lay preacher there, and very upright. She obviously knows he wouldn't approve of Terry and she's scared to say anything. . . ."

" I can see her point," Ashe said.

" So can I, but it's a bit worrying. . . . The question arises whether *we* ought to tell them. Of course, she's over age, she's twenty-two or says she is—but we do feel rather *in loco parentis*—and it's quite a responsibility having one's maid going around with a tough ex-convict who's still very much on trial. . . . Alternatively, we could get rid of her—but that seems harsh. What do you think? "

Ashe said at once, " I think it would have a terribly bad effect on Terry if you did anything at all to try and break it up—just when he's getting his first big lift. . . ." He frowned, thinking for a moment of what Mavis had already said, and wishing she hadn't, since it was sure to reach Terry's ears. " And if the girl's twenty-two,". he added, " it really is up to her, isn't it? One can't arrange other people's lives. . . ."

Winter smiled. " Unless they're ex-prisoners? "

" That's another matter. . . . Anyhow, I should certainly wait for a bit and see how they get on."

Winter nodded slowly. " Well, I must say that's rather my own feeling, too. I'll have to talk to Mavis, but I expect she'll come round if I put it to her in your way. . . . After all, this could be the turning point for young Terry."

" From the look of him," Ashe said, " I think it has been."

Once she had got over her first annoyance, Mavis Winter behaved quite sensibly. She still thought the affair unwise, and Sheila a foolish girl, but she agreed to wait and see how things turned out. According to Terry, who had taken a sharp dislike to her because of what she'd said about him, she knew damn' well she wouldn't get another maid as good as Sheila—and Ashe thought there was some truth in that. But Mavis was mollified, too, by a sort of bargain that Laurence

Winter managed to persuade Sheila to accept—that if he and Mavis facilitated the courtship, which would mean a lot to the young people in opportunities to meet, Sheila would go up and see her parents later in the year and—in spite of her reluctance—tell them about Terry.

As the weeks went by, everything seemed to show that the advice Ashe had given had been sound and that his confidence in Terry was justified. The country wooing, now accepted by all, appeared to be proceeding happily and normally. The couple were constantly out cycling together and had plans—which Ashe thought a trifle ambitious—to get the motor-bike that Terry had set his heart on, so they could go farther afield. In the evenings they often went to the pictures or to a dance in Laybridge. In fact they spent all their spare time together, except for the occasional week-end when the Winters went off to their boat and took Sheila with them. As Mavis said, she could hardly be left behind on her own.

Terry, in this period, seemed quite transformed. It was as though, Ashe thought, a rather dreary plant had suddenly come to spectacular flowering. Ashe was delighted—but not in the least surprised. He had always believed that warmth and friendship and belonging to someone would put the boy on his feet. As things continued to go smoothly all through August, he began to feel that as far as this particular ex-prisoner was concerned his work was over. He saw him only rarely now, for Terry's time was fully taken up with Sheila. When Ashe met Winter, he no longer bothered to ask for a progress report. It wasn't necessary. . . .

Then, early in September, there was a sudden, sharp setback.

It was a Friday evening—a particularly light-hearted one in the Ashe household. First thing in the morning they were due to leave for a week's camping holiday on the South Coast. The animal hutches had been emptied and the Siamese cat boarded out; arrangements had been made for Ashe's fellow vet, Hargreaves, to look after the practice; the six visitees at the prison had been told that Ashe was going away for a short holiday, so that they wouldn't feel let down; the camping gear had all been squeezed into the car. The weather forecast was fine and warm. Everything was set, and Ashe and Nancy were greatly looking forward to the break.

Then, around six o'clock, there was a phone call from Laurence Winter. Could he come over and see Ashe, he asked—it was most urgent. He sounded very disturbed indeed. Ashe told him to come right away and he arrived in less than fifteen minutes, in a state of considerable agitation.

"Thank goodness I managed to catch you before you left," he said. "I'm afraid something very unpleasant has happened. . . . My garage manager, Atkins, reported this afternoon what seems to have been an attempt to break into a drawer of the desk in the office. There's the mark of a sharp tool near the lock—it's quite clear someone's tried to force it."

Ashe gazed at him in dismay.

"Usually," Winter said, "the money we take for petrol is kept in the kiosk in the forecourt until the evening, to save a lot of running about, but when there's a big ' take ' in the morning the cash is moved at lunch-time for safety and locked up in a cash-box in a locked drawer in the office. The office itself isn't locked because the telephone is there. The staff all know of this arrangement. . . . Atkins's view is that someone took a preliminary crack at the drawer, to test its strength, and was interrupted, and decided the whole thing was too risky. . . ."

" You're thinking of Terry, I suppose."

" Well, I'm most reluctant to believe it, especially after the way things have been going—but naturally I thought of it. . . . Who wouldn't? "

" Are the marks fresh? "

" No, not very. It could have happened some time ago—the damage isn't all that noticeable. And theoretically it could have been done by anyone. Any of the staff. There was the chap who left just before Terry came—it could have been him. But I've never had any reason to distrust any of them. . . ."

" What have you done about it? "

" Well, nothing yet—I wanted to see you first. . . . Unfortunately I wasn't there when Atkins made the discovery and the news got around at the garage before I could stop it. Atkins mentioned it to the foreman and they both examined the lock and then the foreman asked the chaps if anyone knew anything about it, and of course that started trouble right away. Apparently they all looked at Terry. He wasn't actually accused, but he was as good as. And he turned really nasty— I've never seen him as he was when I got there. I thought for a moment he was going to hit me when I started asking questions. ' If you think you're going to pin this job on me,' he said, ' you've got another bloody think coming.' He looked really vicious."

" If he thought he was being suspected of something he hadn't done," Ashe said, " he'd naturally be resentful. . . . More than most people. . . ."

" Oh, yes, I realise that."

" And there isn't actually any evidence against him."

" Not a scrap—apart from his record. . . . But the fact that he's an ex-prisoner is going to be quite enough for some of the men—it'll be a job to get them to work with him after this. . . . Honestly, Ashe, I'm wondering if I'll be able to keep him on."

Ashe looked appalled. " But if he didn't do it?—and I don't believe for a moment he did——"

" I know—it would be damned unfair. But what can I do, if the men won't have him? It's a hell of a difficult situation."

" Well, don't for heaven's sake do anything hasty," Ashe said. " I can see you're in a difficult position—but it may not be as bad as you think. . . . And Terry's whole future depends on you now."

" That's the devil of it. . . . You don't suppose I'm not aware of it? "

" After all," Ashe said, " nothing was stolen—the lock wasn't actually broken. You say yourself it could have happened ages ago. . . . You could probably talk the men round—tell them you think it's an old job and that you don't suspect anyone there. . . . I should think it might easily blow over."

" Perhaps," Winter said. He looked very troubled. " But suppose Terry *did* do it? The possibility's there, isn't it? Suppose he tries something else? I can't pretend I feel the same confidence in him to-day as I did yesterday—and I don't think you would if you'd seen the way he looked. We could have been mistaken in him. . . . Still, I won't do anything hasty—I'll think it over. Mavis and I are going up to the boat till Wednesday, so I'll have plenty of time. . . . When will you be back? "

" Next Saturday."

" Well, I'll try and hang on till then—and we'll see what happens."

" And you'll keep Terry on in the meantime? "

" Yes, I'll tell Atkins everything's to go on as usual till I've reached a decision. He's very loyal and reliable, and the men trust him."

Ashe nodded gratefully. " I'm sure you won't regret it. . . . By the way, has Terry talked to Sheila about this, do you know? "

" No—she went up to Northumberland this morning—this is the week-end she's supposed to be telling her parents about him! It seemed a good opportunity as we were going to take some extra days—now it's just another complication. . . . Lord, what a mess! "

" It's a pity she's away," Ashe said. " Terry must be needing her pretty badly just now. . . . I suppose she won't be coming back till you do? "

" No, not till Wednesday or Thursday."

" M'm . . ." Ashe sat frowning. " You know, I think perhaps I'd better try and have a word with him myself. . . ."

Terry was just coming out of the cottage gate with

his bicycle when, half an hour later, Ashe turned up the track. His shoulders were hunched, his face was sullen—and when he saw Ashe it remained sullen. For a moment it seemed as though he was going to push past the car without stopping.

Ashe got out quickly and planted himself in the path. " Hallo, Terry," he said. " I hoped I'd catch you. . . . I hear there's been a bit of trouble at the garage."

Terry stopped, because he had to. " That's right," he said tonelessly. For the first time, Ashe could see what Nancy had meant about eyes like pebbles. " Someone tried to bust open a drawer. That bastard Winter reckons it was me."

" Did he accuse you? "

" He didn't have to—I could see it in his face. Give a dog a bad name! Christ, I was a bloody fool to think I could live that lot down. They all reckon I done it. I guess you do too."

" I don't think anything of the sort," Ashe said sharply. " I don't think you *are* a bloody fool—and if you'd done that you would have been. . . . Look, Terry, this is a setback and I'm damned sorry it's happened—but it has, and you've just got to take it on the chin. We always knew your record would take a bit of time to live down—and so far you've had it pretty smooth. Now you're going to have it rough for a while—but you'll get over it. So don't look so bloody sorry for yourself."

" It's easy to talk. . . ." With a scowl, Terry started to push by.

" Terry, I know how you feel—in your place I'd be resentful, too. I'd be as mad as hell with everyone. But they can't help it—and it won't last. It's a passing trouble."

" Winter's got it in for me. He'll sack me."

" I'm not at all sure he will. He hasn't decided. I think I may be able to persuade him not to. . . ."

Terry met his gaze with a closed face. He seemed, Ashe thought, to have reverted—he looked now as he'd looked at the very start of their acquaintance— hostile, ugly, black. For the moment, all contact with him had been lost. . . . Ashe felt the pedal of the bicycle pressing harshly against his leg, and stepped back.

" I don't want yer bloody charity, Mr. Ashe," Terry said. " I'm sick of bloody sympathy, see. And I'm sick of that perishing bastard *and* his bloody bitch of a wife. . . . I've learned one thing—you got to look arter yerself in this world. *And* I can."

With that, he pushed past, threw a leg over his bicycle, and cycled away. Ashe didn't attempt to follow him. For the moment, there seemed nothing more to be said.

It was a bad start for the holiday. Ashe felt deeply worried—about Terry's future, about the state he'd left him in, about everything. Even if the incident did finally blow over, it would take a long while to get him back on an even keel again. And his present attitude wasn't going to make things any easier for Laurence Winter. If he went on being defiant and abusive, the sack was inevitable. . . . And, of course, there was always the outside chance that he *had* tried to break the lock—that he was angry and resentful because he'd been found out, not because he was

innocent. As Winter had said, it wasn't impossible. . . .
There were things that Ashe couldn't put out of his
mind, however hard he tried. . . . Terry, on his way
to the Ashes' house for the first time, saying, " You
should see the dough they take at the pumps." And
his almost obsessive longing for a motor-bike, which
he couldn't really afford, even on the H.P. . . . The
tiny doubt continued to nag.

Ashe talked quite a lot to Nancy about it. She saw
how upset he was, and she couldn't have been more
understanding—but it wasn't understanding that Ashe
wanted. He wanted reassurance—and where Terry
was concerned he knew he couldn't expect that from
Nancy. In the end, in order not to spoil the holiday
completely, he dropped the subject.

As fine day followed fine day, and the children took
on a deeper shade of brown, and Ashe was able to
swim with Nancy and relax in the sun, his natural
optimism began to return. Probably things would
work out all right in the end—they usually did. Anyway, it was stupid to go on worrying about a situation
over which he had almost no control. And Terry, after
all, was only a small part of his life. . . .

By the Thursday morning, the weight had largely
lifted from his mind. The weather was as beautiful as
ever. The sea, showing through the V of the downs
where they were camped, was blue and placid. Sitting
beside the tent, puffing at his pipe and helping young
Margaret to wash up after breakfast while Nancy went
off to the camp store to shop, he hadn't a fault to find
with anything—not even the kids!

Someone's dachshund bitch came waddling up, her
belly almost touching the ground, her nose white with

age. Automatically, Ashe's hand went out to stroke her. " She's old, isn't she? " he said.

Jane looked at him solemnly. " Is that why her legs are worn down? " she asked.

Ashe gave a huge guffaw—the first for days.

It was cut off short as Nancy suddenly returned. She had a newspaper in her hand. Her face was a sickly yellow under its tan. " Robert," she said. " Oh, *Robert* . . .! "

He took one look at her and grabbed the paper she was holding out.

There was a large photograph of Mavis Winter on the front page. Beside it was another photograph, of Terry Booth, with a detailed description of him underneath it. The accompanying story said :

" To escape the discomfort of a night in a grounded boat, a woman returned alone to her house in Sussex —and met her death at the hands of an intruder.

The woman, Mrs. Mavis Winter, 53, of Hilltop, Shedley, was found strangled yesterday afternoon in a field behind the house. With her husband, Mr. Laurence Winter, she had been spending a few days on their cabin cruiser in Essex, but after the boat had stranded on a mud bank on Monday she decided to go home.

Her body was found yesterday by Mr. Winter when he returned to Sussex. The house had been broken into, and it is thought that Mrs. Winter may have been attacked while chasing the intruder.

Investigations are in the hands of Inspector Arthur Mayo, of the East Sussex C.I.D. The police believe that a twenty-four-year-old motor mechanic named

Terry Booth, employed at Mr. Winter's garage near Shedley, may be able to help them with their inquiries, and are anxious to interview him. Booth is reported to have been missing from his home for some days. Anyone able to give information as to his whereabouts is asked to get in touch with the Chief Constable of East Sussex, or with any police station. . . ."

II

SOME NINETY minutes later Ashe was being shown into
the small, bare office at Laybridge police station where
Inspector Arthur Mayo had set up his temporary head-
quarters for the Winter case. Ashe already knew Mayo
slightly, having had a couple of semi-official contacts
with him in connection with his prison work. The
inspector was a grim, greying man, nearing retirement
and looking as though he wouldn't be sorry when he
reached it. His expression seemed always to be on the
verge of a scowl, but this was because of his heavy,
saturnine brows and the downward, mastiff-like sag of
all the lower parts of his face. He was sardonic, but not
in fact bad-tempered. He half rose as Ashe entered.

" Hullo, Mr. Ashe," he said, shaking hands. " Have
a seat, will you? " Ashe drew out the wooden chair
opposite him. Mayo's manner was polite rather than
welcoming. As prison visitor and sponsor to Booth,
Ashe could be considered to have a special relationship
to the case, and must therefore be spared a little time.
" Well," he said, " it looks as though your young
protégé has let you down pretty badly."

" Have you found him yet? "

" Not yet."

" Tell me what happened, Inspector."

Mayo sat back. " Well, I can only give you the story
as far as we've been able to piece it together. . . . You
know, of course, that Mr. Winter and his wife went off

59

on Saturday for a long week-end on their boat. And you've probably read that on the Monday they got into a bit of trouble with it—ran aground on a shoaling bank. Mrs. Winter didn't fancy the prospect of spending a night at an angle of forty-five degrees, so she decided to come home. She drove herself back on the Monday evening. Winter got the boat off the mud with a bit of help, spent Tuesday cruising around, and came back yesterday. He found his house in chaos. The lock of the back door had been forced and the door was ajar. There was a trail of slashing through the ground floor of the house—kitchen, dining-room, sitting-room, study. In the study, a picture covering a small wall safe had been taken down and there were tool marks round the safe as though a start had been made at prising it out bodily. In the kitchen there was some dirty crockery and the remains of a meal. Upstairs, Mrs. Winter's bed had been slept in and not re-made. That was the scene. . . ."

Mayo paused for a moment to put a light to his pipe.

" There was no sign of Mrs. Winter," he went on. " Mr. Winter rang the local police and they went round straight away. A constable at an upper window noticed what looked like an electric hand lamp in the grass beside a path that runs up through the paddock. He investigated, and it *was* a lamp. He and Winter started looking around, and very soon they came on Mrs. Winter's body. It was half hidden in the long grass near the right-hand hedge. She was wearing a night-dress, dressing-gown and bedroom slippers. She'd been strangled with great violence. . . ."

"Ghastly," Ashe said. He sat for a moment in shocked

silence. " When do you suppose it happened—on the Monday night? "

Mayo nodded. " That's what the various signs around the house indicate—and it squares with the medical report. Evidently Mrs. Winter got back, cooked herself a light supper, and went to bed. Some time in the night the intruder broke in, made his way to the study, and started to work on the safe. Before he could get very far, the noise roused Mrs. Winter. She put on her dressing-gown and slippers and went downstairs. The intruder heard her coming and ran out through the back door and up the paddock path. Mrs. Winter grabbed the hand lamp—I gather it was always kept on the window ledge in the hall—and went after him. She must have been a very courageous woman. The intruder stopped and turned on her, strangled her, and then carried her body into the long grass to hide it. . . . Anyway, that's our reconstruction at the moment."

" What about the dog? " Ashe asked. " They had a big boxer."

" They'd put it in kennels for the week-end," Mayo said. " Apparently they always did that when they went on the boat."

Ashe nodded. " When did Terry Booth disappear? "

" Yesterday evening. He was around as usual till then—working at the garage, taking his midday meal at the Dysons'. He was last seen at the White Hart at Laybridge about seven o'clock, by a Shedley man who'd heard we were wanting to talk to him, and told him so. Booth said he'd come and see us, and instead he cleared off. It looks as though he thought at first he could brazen it out, and then his nerve failed."

" Is there any direct evidence against him, Inspector? Any fingerprints? "

" No. . . . Whoever did it wore gloves—which is what Booth would certainly have done. He knew enough for that when he did the warehouse job."

" Any footprints? "

" No. . . . We did hope for something useful there, because the paddock's just been limed—not that the stuff would take prints very well, it's too thin on the ground, but there seemed a chance. . . . Then it turned out that the liming was done *after* the murder—Winter left instructions with a local contractor to do it on the Tuesday while he was away—so the lime was a hindrance rather than a help. . . . In any case, I'm afraid there was a lot of trampling around by other people both before and after the body was discovered, so the picture's hopelessly confused. . . ."

Ashe was frowning. " If a man was working in the paddock after the murder, how was it he didn't see the body—or the lamp? "

" Because, as I said, they were in the long grass and close to the edge of the field. The constable happened to spot the lamp because he was high up. . . . The contractor must have passed quite near to both of them, the lime shows that—but obviously not near enough."

" I see. . . ." Ashe took up his thread again. " Well, if there's no direct evidence against Booth, couldn't the intruder have been someone else? "

Mayo gave a dismissive shrug. " Booth's cleared off. . . . And all the indirect evidence points to him."

" His record, you mean? Robbery with violence—the same type of case."

"Not only that, Mr. Ashe—there are lots of other pointers. The office-breaking incident at the garage, for one—I gather you know about that. There was an ugly row, Winter tells me. . . . It looks as though Booth thought he'd be sacked and decided to try and line his pocket and clear off while the going was good— only the plan went wrong. . . . There's the slashing, too—he obviously carved things up as he went in, very deliberately. . . . Sheer spite—and it goes with the mood he was in."

Ashe gave a deep sigh. It did, indeed!—more even than the inspector realised.

"And that's not all," Mayo went on. "This job was done by someone with a great deal of inside know-ledge—of the house, the family, the set-up, everything. Not by any stranger. And Booth had the knowledge."

"What exactly are you thinking of?"

"Well, to start with, whoever did it must have be-lieved the house was empty—otherwise he wouldn't have made such a row. He'd have sneaked in quietly, not forced a lock—and he wouldn't have rampaged around inside the way he did. Booth would have known the family was away for the week-end—he'd have heard it from his girl friend, Sheila MacLean, if from nowhere else. . . . Then whoever did it must have known about the safe behind the picture—the intruder went straight to it after the slashing, nothing else was touched. Booth might well have heard about the safe from Sheila—or he could have discovered it himself on one of his visits. . . . And, of course, there's the fact that the killing took place at all. It looks to me as though Mrs. Winter was killed because of that lamp she was carrying—it throws a powerful beam and she'd have had a good view of the intruder if she'd caught him in it. I think he *was* caught in it, and knew he'd been recognised. As Booth would have been. So he had to kill her, or be jailed for the break-in. The killing makes no sense otherwise. Any active man could have got away from a woman in a dressing-gown and slippers. . . ."

The thought crossed Ashe's mind that Terry had had a grudge against Mavis Winter anyway—but he kept it to himself. Instead, he said, " There must have been other people who knew that the Winters were away— the tradesmen, the Dysons, the garage staff. . . ." He knew he was clutching at straws, but he felt driven to do what he could. " Other people may have known about the safe. Other people would have been recognised in the light beam, too."

" I dare say," Mayo said grimly, " but I think we'll find when we check that they all spent the night snugly in bed. Most people do. . . . Booth, as he lives alone, could have been in and out of his cottage without anyone knowing. . . . No, I'm afraid the chances of an alternative intruder can be pretty well ruled out. Another man might fit some of the circumstances, but not all. With Booth, there's his past record, his motive, his opportunity, his knowledge—everything. Surely you agree? "

" I'm not left with much choice," Ashe said.

" Exactly. . . . Anyway, we'll soon learn the truth when we find him. These young hoodlums are tough enough when they're with a gang or beating up some defenceless woman, but once they're on their own they usually crack. My guess is he'll break down and talk. . . . I suppose you haven't any suggestions as to where he might have made for? "

Ashe shook his head. " There's nowhere I can think of. As far as I know he'd lost touch with all his old cronies. . . . In fact he'd scarcely a friend in the world except Sheila MacLean."

Mayo grunted. " Well, he didn't go to her—she's been interviewed at her home up north and she doesn't seem to know anything. . . . It's bad luck for her, getting mixed up with a fellow like that. . . . Bad luck for you too, Mr. Ashe, after all the work you put in on him."

" It's one hell of a thing all round," Ashe said. " For everyone. How's Laurence Winter? How's he taken it? "

" He seems hardly to know what's hit him yet."

" Poor devil. . . . Are your chaps still at the house? "

" No, we've finished for the moment—he's on his own there."

Ashe nodded. " Then I'd better go and see him."

" I think he'd be glad to see you," Mayo said. He got up from behind his desk. " You know, you mustn't take this too hard, Mr. Ashe—about young Booth, I mean. You visitors do your best, but you can't expect to turn a vicious lout into a good citizen by kindness. Some of these fellows are quite incorrigible. . . . Personally I'm against all this modern softness with young criminals—there's too much binding over and not enough bending over, if you ask me."

" Perhaps you'd like the thumbscrews back," Ashe said.

" I'd like a lot more severity, Mr. Ashe, and that's the truth. All this cosseting in prison—cinema shows, newspapers, tobacco, friendly understanding visitors

—where does it get us? More attacks on warders, more
break-outs, more crime. . . . You've got to put fear
into these young thugs that prey on society, it's the
only thing that'll ever stop them. Welfare workers and
psychologists won't. . . . Still, that's just my unofficial
view."

Ashe gave a curt nod. He was very ready to discuss
penology with the inspector, but not just now. " I
wonder if you'd give Laurence Winter a ring," he said,
" and tell him I'm on my way. . . ."

He drove at a slow pace to Shedley, sunk in moody
reflection and hardly noticing the road. This whole day
was an unrelieved ordeal for him. The shock and
horror of the morning's news was still very much with
him. Seeing Winter would be as hard as anything he
had done in his life. It wasn't as though this was an
ordinary visit of sympathy. Ashe's own responsibility
for what had happened weighed on him intolerably.
Almost single-handed, he'd made it possible. . . .

The worst moment was waiting for the door to
open, waiting for the first glimpse of the stricken man,
not knowing what bitterness, what reproaches there
might be. The reality was as bad as he'd feared—but
in a different way. Mayo had been right—Winter
looked more dazed than anything. Pathetic in his
bewilderment, in his gratitude at Ashe's call, in the
limpness of his handshake.

Ashe said, " We heard the news at nine, Laurence.
. . . It's so dreadful I simply don't know what to
say. . . ."

" I still can't believe it," Winter said. " It's like a
nightmare. . . ." His face quivered. " Robert, she

looked so awful—I could hardly recognise her. . . .
I'll never be able to forget it. . . ." With an effort that
was painful to see, he controlled himself. " Would you
like some whisky?—I've had some. . . . It blunts things
a bit."

Ashe shook his head. " I feel it's all my fault," he
said. " I brought it on you. . . . I wish to God I'd never
set eyes on Booth."

" Yes," Winter said, " so do I. . . . But you mustn't
blame yourself. I admit I felt bitter last night—when
I thought how nearly I didn't take him on—how you
persuaded me. . . . But the feeling's gone—I know it's
not fair. You were completely frank—and it was my
decision. You told me there was a risk. . . . Though
heaven knows I never thought of anything like this.
. . . It's incredible. . . ." For a moment he stood staring
into space. " It could so easily not have happened,
too. . . . That damned boat! You know, I wanted
Mavis to put up at the pub there, but she was a bit
fed up with the trouble we'd had, she said she'd sooner
come home. She was always independent, and she
knew how to look after herself—it never occurred to
me for a moment that anything could happen. And
then—*this*. . . ."

" Dreadful," Ashe murmured.

" It was such a shock. . . . I'd rung the house on
Tuesday, and there wasn't a reply, but I didn't worry,
I thought she was probably out shopping. When
I got home I still didn't worry—both cars were
in the garage—everything looked normal. But the
house! You haven't seen the mess. Come and have a
look. . . ."

He led the way through the rooms. Ashe stood

aghast at the malice of the destruction. Chair seats had been slashed, curtains savagely ripped down, the dining-room table deeply scored, the front of a mahogany bureau criss-crossed with scratches.

" The police think he used the same tool for the slashing as for forcing the door," Winter said. " Something like a big sharpened tyre lever—but they haven't been able to find it. . . . I suppose he could have taken something from the garage and put it back afterwards. . . ."

He showed Ashe the safe, the bits of plaster dug out of the wall around it, the picture that had covered it— its glass now smashed, its canvas torn. " It must have sounded like an earthquake upstairs," he said. " If only there'd been a phone there—but neither of us had ever felt the need of one. . . . Or if she'd just stayed in bed. . . . If only, if only . . . ! "

" Was there much in the safe? " Ashe asked.

" Not much—about a hundred pounds in cash that we kept as a stand-by in case we ran out when the banks were shut. And a few papers. . . ."

" Do you think Sheila knew there was money there? "

" She might have seen one of us putting it in or taking it out—but I wouldn't have thought so. It didn't happen very often. . . . She knew the safe was there, of course—and a safe's a safe. There's usually something in it. . . . Anyway, the money was only part of it. . . ." Winter gazed around at the chaos. " How that fellow must have hated me! You'd imagine I'd done him some harm, instead of helping him all I could. . . . The ironical thing is, I'd practically made up my mind to give him the benefit of the doubt about

that office-breaking, and see him through in the job.
. . . And this is what I get!"

They went through the kitchen to the back door.
There was the deep mark of an iron instrument where
it had been thrust into the wood near the lock and
used as a lever. The lock had been almost forced off
its screws. The bolts at the top and bottom of the
door hadn't been shot, and were intact. "It was a good
lock," Winter said, "you can see that. . . . He must
have gone at it like a madman. . . ."

They walked out to the edge of the paddock, white
now with its coating of fine, powdered lime. Winter
pointed up the grass path that skirted the rough verge.
"That's where the lamp was—just off the path to the
right. Mavis was over there—farther to the right.
. . . We won't go up, if you don't mind—no point in
getting this stuff on your shoes. . . ."

Ashe nodded understandingly. They turned away.

"What are you going to do, Laurence?" Ashe said.
"Have you any plans?"

Winter shook his head. "I'm just taking things as
they come. . . . There'll be the inquest, of course—
the funeral. . . . I'll have to get through that somehow.
. . . I can't really think about anything. I don't want
to think. That's probably why I keep on talking all
the time. . . . I'm glad you came, Robert, it's been a
relief to talk to you. . . . I suppose I'll have to do something about Sheila when she gets back. . . . I think I'll
send her to sleep at Mrs. Dyson's, and have her up
just in the daytime till I decide what to do. . . . Poor
girl, it must have been a frightful shock for her, too—
a double shock. . . . *I* don't know. . . ." He passed a

hand wearily over his face. " It just doesn't seem possible."

" If there's anything Nancy and I can do to help . . ."

" That's good of you, Robert—I'll let you know if there is. But I expect I'll be able to cope. I've got to occupy myself. . . ."

They walked slowly along the path to the garage. The garden was soft with autumn purples, the grass still wet with the morning dew, the tree tops motionless. Tranquillity lay over everything. It was hard to think of violence there, of murder. . . .

" Mavis loved this place," Winter said. " She was really happy here. We both were. . . . Now it seems so empty I can hardly bear the sight of it. . . ."

They stopped at Ashe's car. Winter opened the door for him. " Thank you again for coming," he said. " I know it can't have been easy for you. . . . We'll be in touch."

He raised his hand in a silent gesture of farewell as Ashe drove away.

Ashe returned to the seaside camp that afternoon in an even unhappier frame of mind than before he'd seen Winter. Almost, he wished that he *had* been blamed. If Winter had cursed him to hell and thrown him out —which Ashe felt he would have done himself if the positions had been reversed—that at least would have seemed natural and healthy. But Winter's unfocused, sleep-walking euphoria, his almost maudlin readiness to forgive Ashe for the irreparable harm he'd caused, the fact that he hadn't even denounced Terry in unbridled terms—all this made the situation worse. To Ashe it was evidence of deep-seated, paralysing injury—

a numbness which was infinitely more disturbing than anger would have been. No doubt it would pass—but that gave little consolation to Ashe at the moment.

His report to Nancy was meagre. He told her, briefly, what Mayo had told him—the known events, the deadly reconstruction. He told her of his talk with Winter, and described the scene at the house. But that was all. He was too shaken by the tragedy, too upset by his own fatal misjudgment of Terry, to want to discuss it yet. Never in his life had he felt so depressed. Nancy wasn't in a much better state. The shattering news had left her utterly drained. Though the Winters hadn't become intimates of the Ashes, they'd been close enough for the impact of the murder to be personal and crushing. Silence, inward-turned and brooding, lay over the family camp that evening like a pall. Nancy would have suggested curtailing the holiday and going home if the children hadn't been looking forward to their last day on the sands— and if there'd been any hope that things would seem better at home. But there was no reason why they should. . . .

It wasn't until the following morning, when Nancy was beginning to recover from the first shock and Ashe had had time to think things over, that they talked at any length about the crime. Nancy put the common-sense point of view about her husband's responsibility. Anything like remorse on his part, she said, would be quite idiotic. He had merely done his job—a difficult job—and everyone made mistakes. Laurence wasn't a child and he must take responsibility for his own decisions—as he was quite ready to do. He'd had a cruel stroke of luck, and she was deeply sorry for him—but to dwell on him would be silly. . . . As for Terry, he was just beyond words. . . .

Ashe nodded his agreement. There could be no possible excuse for Terry. But his tone, when he talked about him, was more bewildered than bitter.

" Quite apart from anything else," he said, " you'd think he'd have had more sense than to go and break in there. . . . How stupid can you get, for Pete's sake! He was bound to be suspected after what had happened —everything was stacked against him. . . . And the slashing was practically a signature."

" You've often said that most criminals are stupid," Nancy reminded him.

" They often are—but I thought Terry was an exception."

" I know—you always saw more in him than anyone else could——" She broke off, as thin ice cracked all round her. " But it *was* in character, you know—the stupidity, I mean. . . . When he broke into that warehouse he took a big risk for almost nothing. . . . He's obviously quite reckless."

" What he did this time wasn't just reckless," Ashe said, " it was practically suicidal. From first to last. . . . Look at the way he stuck around for two days before clearing off. Why didn't he go at once, and give himself a long start? It's all very well to say he meant to try and brazen it out, and then changed his mind when things started to get hot—but how could he ever have thought it was possible to brazen it out, with so much against him? "

Nancy was silent for a while, trying to work it out.

" It must have been a choice of evils for him," she

said at last. " After all, running away is practically a
confession of guilt—there's not much hope if you're
caught. . . . As long as you stay put, you can always
deny everything and hope there'll be no proof. . . . I
should think he must have been in quite a state after
the murder—which he wouldn't have intended to
commit—and a man who's suddenly afraid he may be
hanged can't be judged by rational standards. He probably didn't know *what* to do—so he did nothing. . . ."

" Until his nerve broke? "

" Yes."

Ashe grunted. " Well, it's an explanation of sorts.
. . ." He picked up the newspaper in a dissatisfied way,
and put it down again. He'd read all there was about
the case—which was very little. There was still no
news of Terry.

" I wonder where he is," he said.

Terry Booth was a long way away—more than two
hundred miles from the scene of the crime. It was the
farthest from London he'd ever been. To begin with
he'd felt that all that distance was somehow on his
side. Just to be on the move, with the miles rolling
away behind him, had cheered him up a lot. But he
didn't feel that way now. Now he was stuck. . . .

The first night had been easy—the night he'd cleared
off. There hadn't been any description of him out
then. He'd had a pound or so in his pocket. He'd
known the best place to make for—he'd learned that
in jug from blokes who'd tried it and wished they'd
stayed there. . . . He'd had no trouble hitching lifts,
especially after he'd got into the stream of north-going
lorry traffic. No trouble with the drivers, either—to

them he'd been just another fellow moving to a new job. The trip had taken him all night, but he'd made it. . . .

Then—daylight in a strange city. A quick look at someone's newspaper—and he'd seen his own face there. He'd expected that—but not so soon. The cops had moved fast. He hadn't thought his scar would show up so much in a picture, either. Everyone would be looking out for that scar. Any second someone might grab him. . . . He'd started to walk, pulling his cap well down, keeping his face turned away when he passed anyone close. He'd have to find a quiet spot to lie up in. It wasn't even safe to buy food. Not till after dark. . . .

He'd walked out of the city and spent the day hidden among some bushes beside a canal towpath. At dusk, aching with hunger, he'd gone back in and bought some pies at a street coffee stall near the docks, keeping well back in the shadows, not saying much. He'd wolfed a couple of them on the spot, washing them down with a mug of tea, and pocketed the rest for later. Afterwards he'd walked round the outside of the docks, past the dock gates. He'd seen the dock police looking at everyone who went in, stopping everyone they didn't know. He'd never get by them, whatever story he told—not with his scar. But that was the way out all right—the only way out for him. He could see the ferry boat tied up there now, its gangway down and no one standing by it. Loading up for its regular night trip. If he could only get inside those gates, it wouldn't be too hard to slip aboard and hide. . . .

He'd walked up and down, eyeing the gates, think-ing maybe there'd be a chance to nip past when the police were busy with someone else. But there hadn't been. He'd walked all around the high dock fence, looking for a broken bit, for some place he could climb —but he hadn't found one. He'd need a ladder to get over that lot. . . . What a hope!

He'd seen the ferry leave, and he'd still stuck around, watching the comings and goings, sizing the place up. . . . Then, as daylight got near, he'd gone back to his canal bank. He'd eaten the food he'd brought away from the coffee stall, and he'd slept, his coat drawn over his head. He'd slept for hours. . . .

Now he was awake. He felt very scruffy. In a couple of days his unshaven face would start looking different from the picture. The scar wouldn't be so easy to see. But he couldn't wait that long. In another day his money would run out. Somehow, he'd got to get away that night. If he didn't, he'd be caught for sure. And if they caught him, they'd top him. . . . For capital murder. . . .

As soon as it was dark, he tried again. He'd had an idea, lying there on the canal bank. He wasn't finished yet—he'd show them. . . . Opposite the dock gates, there were traffic lights at a T-junction. He'd seen lorries waiting there before going on into the docks. It might work. . . .

He reached the lights at ten o'clock. He was hungry again, and thirsty, but he didn't dare risk the coffee stall a second time. He found an automatic milk machine outside a shop and drank some milk. He felt better after that. He started to walk up and down the pavement by the lights. There were a few people about but he kept out of their way and they didn't take any notice of him. He walked smartly as though he was going somewhere—he didn't want to be picked up for loitering. All the time he watched for a lorry, ready to make for it if the lights went red as it got to them. It was half an hour before one stopped—and then there was a car, right behind it. . . . He walked on, up and down. Nothing came, only cars. The lights winked and changed. . . . Then a big lorry came grinding up and stopped at the red. Terry gave a quick look round. There was no one near. The lorry was loaded with wooden crates. The back was open and a rope hung down. Terry heaved himself up as the lights changed and climbed in over the crates till he was deep inside. . . .

Now—would it go into the docks? If it didn't, he'd have to slip off at the next lights it stopped at, and try again. He held his breath. . . . Yes, it was going straight across to the gates. It pulled up just inside. He heard voices. Slow footsteps at the back of the lorry. . . . Then they moved away. The lorry went on. Very slowly, now. Round a corner and along the waterfront. Bumping over a rail track. . . . At a place that seemed darker than most, Terry dropped off. . . .

The camping holiday was over. Early on the Saturday morning the Ashe family packed up their tent and equipment and drove home. They had hardly been back in the house five minutes when the telephone rang. It was Inspector Mayo.

" Hullo, Mr. Ashe," he said. " I've been trying to get you for some time. . . . You've heard about Booth, I suppose."

" No. . . ."

"Oh, I thought you would have done—it was on the radio this morning. . . . Well, he's been picked up." Mayo sounded unusually cheerful.

"Where?"

"Liverpool. He'd managed to get into the docks somehow and was trying to stow away on the Dublin boat. The watch spotted him as he went up the gangway, and that was that. . . . It was a pretty stupid attempt—he never had a chance, of course. . . ."

Ashe grunted. "So what happens now?"

"Well," Mayo said, "he's being brought down by train—I'm not sure yet when he'll be arriving. But he'll definitely be here by this evening and I wondered if you'd care to look in. Laybridge police station. . . . I don't expect much difficulty with him, but in case he proves stubborn it might be helpful to have you around."

"Very well," Ashe said. "I'll be there about seven."

The inspector was appreciably less cheerful when Ashe saw him at Laybridge that evening. Terry, it appeared, had arrived with his escort shortly after three o'clock and had since been closely questioned—but to no purpose.

"He denies everything, admits nothing," Mayo said. "We've been at him for hours but we can't shake him. He's tougher than I thought. . . . Maybe you can get something out of him."

"I'd like to see him, anyway," Ashe said non-committally.

"Good. . . . I'm just going over to the Dysons' to have a word with Sheila MacLean—I gather she's back. If you're through before I am perhaps you'd wait for me. I shan't be long."

" Yes, I'll wait," Ashe said.

" Right. . . . Sergeant, take Mr. Ashe in, will you."

Ashe followed the sergeant into another small room. A constable was in there with Terry, but he left at a jerk of the sergeant's head. Terry was sitting at a table, hunched forward on his elbows, an empty tea-cup beside him. His clothes were crumpled and dusty, his face was grey and without expression.

Ashe sat down opposite him. " Well? " he said.

Terry regarded him sullenly. " Well *what*? They been over it and over it. Working in shifts. Telling me what I done—trying to put the wind up me. . . . You got to start now? "

" I only wanted to see you and hear what you had to say," Ashe said. " Considering everything, that's reasonable enough, don't you think? "

" I didn't do it—that's all I got to say." Terry moistened his lips with his tongue. Behind the defiant tone, Ashe sensed fear. " I don't know nothink more abaht it than what I read in the papers."

" Then why did you clear off? "

" 'Cos someone told me the cops was lookin' for me and I knew damn' well they'd pin it on me if they could. . . . I was on a pub crawl here in Laybridge, see, Wednesday night and pretty fed up with every-thing. . . . Then a fellow come in what knew me, fellow named Petrie from the village, all full of the murder. First I'd heard abaht it, that was. He said he'd been told the police back in Shedley wanted to talk to me. . . . I arst him what they'd found up at the house—details, like—an' he told me abaht the breaking-in an' how someone had carved the place up an' strangled the old woman. . . ." His tongue flicked round his lips again.

" Go on," Ashe said.

" Well, that was enough for me. With my record, see, and the row with Winter an' everythink, I reckoned I'd be for it. I know the bloody cops, they'll make up the evidence if they haven't got it—frame you as soon as look at you. . . . So I beat it. . . . I wasn't goin' to be strung up for somethink I hadn't done. . . . I was scared, see. . . . I dunno—maybe it wasn't very smart. Maybe I'd of done better to stay. I guess it'll make things worse now. . . . That's what I done, though."

" What were you going to do in Dublin? "

" Get lost, o' course. Whatcher think? "

" What about Sheila? I suppose you were just going to abandon her? "

" No, I wasn't. . . . I was goin' to wait till the heat was off an' then write to her. . . ." His eyes met Ashe's, his glance wavered. " I wouldn't of let her down. . . ." For the first time, he looked like a man with a load on his conscience.

Ashe said, " Where *were* you on Monday night, Terry? "

" Asleep in the cottage, o' course. . . . But I can't prove it, can I? I can't prove nothing."

" Did you know there was money in Winter's safe? "

" Blimey, I didn't know 'e had a safe."

" Sheila didn't mention it? "

" 'Course she didn't. . . . Do you s'pose we'd nothing better to do than talk abaht bloody safes? "

Ashe fell silent. He could see little use in any further catechism, when Mayo and his men must have been all over the ground. He hadn't got anywhere, and he obviously wasn't going to. . . . After a moment he pushed back his chair.

"Any rate," Terry said, sweating, "I'd of had too much bloody sense to do what that fellow done. . . . Rushin' off up the field, 'stead of dodging rahnd the corner of the house an' getting away at the front. . . . Whoever done that job must of been off his nut. . . . *And* I wouldn't strangle anyone, specially a woman. Even if she was a bloody bitch. . . ."

Ashe got up.

Terry's tone suddenly changed. "I didn't do it, Mr. Ashe," he said. "I swear to God I didn't do it. Why can't they give me a break? I don't know no more abaht it than what you do—that's the truth. Someone else done it." He looked straight at Ashe. "Honest!"

His appearance was so genuine, his manner so outraged, that for a moment Ashe felt almost inclined to believe him.

"You always said you was my friend," Terry pressed him. "If you're my friend, you gotta stand by me."

Ashe gazed at him, but said nothing.

Terry's eyes grew hard. "Ain't my word good enough for yer?"

Sadly, Ashe shook his head. "I'm afraid it isn't, Terry—not by itself, not in all the circumstances. . . . My mind isn't closed, but I can't just say I believe you. . . . I wish I could."

"Then you're no bloody good to me," Terry said.

In sudden, futile anger, he swept the cup and saucer with a crash on to the floor. " All that talk—an' then when I get in a spot you turn on me. Fine bloody friend you are—just like all the rest of 'em. . . . Well, —— off, then. I don't need you. I'll fight the b—— on me own."

The constable looked in. " All right, Mr. Ashe? " Terry turned away. With a sigh, Ashe left him.

The sergeant found a chair for him in the outer office and he sat down to wait for Mayo. He had more than enough on his mind to keep him occupied.

The interview, at first merely distressing, had left him baffled and uncertain. Some of the things Terry had said—as well as the way he had said them—had started new and disturbing trains of thought. Questions that hadn't occurred to him before seemed to call for answers. The more he reflected on what was supposed to have happened, the more puzzled he felt about certain aspects of Terry's alleged behaviour.

He was still deep in his problems when, after fifteen minutes or so, the inspector returned.

" Well," Mayo asked, " did you get anything out of him? "

Ashe shook his head. " It was just as you said—a strong denial. A *very* strong denial."

" Yes, he's a glib talker when he gets started."

" He says he cleared off because he thought he'd be blamed for something he hadn't done. . . . You know, of course."

Mayo nodded gloomily. " The usual line. . . ."

" What did Sheila have to say? "

" Nothing helpful. . . . She admitted she knew about

the safe, but says she never mentioned it to Booth. She says she didn't know what was in it."

" How is she? " Ashe asked.

" She's very worried about Booth—wants to see him. But she doesn't give much away. She's a case of still waters, if you ask me. . . ."

" You're not suggesting there was collusion between them? "

Mayo shrugged. " Not really—I've nothing much to go on. But maybe . . . She says she doesn't believe he did it. She's certainly sold on the fellow."

" Yes. . . ." There was a slightly strained pause. Then Ashe said, " Inspector—do you happen to know what Terry's demeanour was like when he went back to the garage after the murder? On the Tuesday morning? "

" If you mean did he behave like a murderer," Mayo said, " I can tell you right away that there aren't any rules."

" Perhaps not, but I'd expect some sort of reaction —some sign of strain. I can't imagine anyone in that position seeming absolutely normal. . . . Was he normal? "

" By all accounts he was glum and silent. And that seems to me to fit all right."

" It fits other things besides murder," Ashe said. " He'd have been glum and silent anyway, I should think, with his mates at the garage suspecting him of attempted theft and the sack hanging over him."

Mayo grunted. " Well, that's true. . . ."

Ashe pressed on. " If by any chance Terry *didn't* do it, Inspector—if, as he says, he didn't know anything at all about it—he might well have behaved as he did,

don't you think? Going back to work gloomy, going off
on solitary pub crawls at night to drown his sorrows,
rushing off in panic when he heard about the murder
and that the police wanted him? Stupid, of course, but
not entirely surprising, considering everything."

Mayo regarded him quizzically. " I suppose you
could look at it that way, Mr. Ashe—though, with
so much else against him, I don't know why you
should."

" Someone's got to act as the prisoner's friend,"
Ashe said. " To tell you the truth, there are several
odd things that have occurred to me. . . . For instance,
the fact that Mrs. Winter was *strangled*."

" What's odd about that? "

" It doesn't seem to fit Terry. On past showing,
he's a fellow who hits out with what he's got—he's a
basher. . . . And he must have had a heavy tool with
him when he rushed out of the house, the one he broke
the lock and did the slashing with, because otherwise
it would have been found. . . . So why didn't he use
it? He'd have had to drop the tool, strangle Mrs.
Winter, then pick the tool up again. Does that make
sense? "

" I think so," Mayo said. " Probably he didn't want
to risk getting blood on him."

" He didn't bother about that when he bashed the
man at the warehouse."

" No—and he's had time to realise his mistake,"
Mayo said grimly. " Nearly three years! These chaps
learn a lot in jail."

" Well—maybe. . . . But take another point. . . .
Terry brought this up himself, or I probably wouldn't
have thought of it. . . . Why would he have rushed

away up the paddock, up a path that didn't lead anywhere except to the top, when he could have nipped
round the corner of the house to the front and got clean
away without any risk of being recognised? It's not
as though he didn't know the ground."

Mayo shrugged. "Criminals who suddenly find
themselves being chased don't always do the sensible
thing," he said. "As often as not they lose their heads.
. . . That's how they get caught."

"If Terry had lost his head to that extent, would he
have thought about the danger of getting blood on
him?"

"M'm—it's hard to say. . . ."

"Well, I don't see that you can have it both ways.
. . . Then there's something else I thought of. . . ."

"You *have* been busy," Mayo said, with a sour
smile.

"I've simply been trying to get the picture straight
in my mind, Inspector. . . . The thing is, I can't understand why the body should have been put in the
long grass. It's pretty clear that Mrs. Winter was
killed on or near the path, because that's where the
lamp was dropped. Now you said the other day that
Terry wanted to hide the body—but what would
have been the point? What would he have gained by
it?"

"He'd have gained a bit of time," Mayo said.
"Time to make up his mind what to do before the
hue and cry started. Time for the scent to get cold.
The longer the delay before discovery, the harder it
usually is for the police to prove a case. . . . He must
have had something like that in mind. For the same
reason, I imagine, he went and pulled the back door

as nearly shut as it would stay, after the killing. Mrs. Winter certainly wouldn't have closed it behind her —and Winter found it only just ajar, you'll remember. . . . I'd call these the ordinary, precautionary measures of a man who wanted to conceal his guilt as long as possible."

" I see. . . ." Ashe sat considering. " It's possible, I suppose. . . . All the same, Inspector, I don't feel you've really explained everything away—not completely."

Mayo wasn't looking entirely satisfied, either. " Well, you can't expect a perfect textbook crime from a man like Booth," he said, in a grumbling tone. "You can't expect everything to make complete sense. And these are fairly small points. . . . I'm quite sure in my own mind that Booth *did* do it."

" Have you checked up on the other people—the ones who had the same sort of knowledge as he had? Managers, staffs, tradesmen, and so on? "

" They've all been interviewed, yes—everyone we could think of. . . . And there isn't much doubt they were all tucked up in bed on the night of the murder."

" Is there *any* doubt? "

" Well, wives can lie—but in this case I'm sure they haven't. There's no hint of a motive with any of these fellows—they're just on the fringe. . . . No, it was Booth all right."

" You're going to charge him, are you? "

" Ah, that's another matter." Gloom settled on Mayo's face again. " It's one thing to feel pretty sure myself—it's quite another to find evidence that'll satisfy a court. We certainly haven't got it yet. . . .

Booth's denied all knowledge of the affair from the beginning, he's got a sort of explanation for running away, we can't prove he *wasn't* at the cottage that night, and there isn't a single piece of material evidence against him. . . . At the moment, we couldn't even get him committed."

" Then what are you going to do? "

" Well, we shall hold him for further questioning— probably over the week-end. In the meantime, we shall try to get the further evidence we need. Someone may have seen or heard something—someone may come forward. All we need is one solid fact. . . ."

" And if you don't get it? "

Mayo shrugged again. " Then I'm afraid we'll have no choice but to let him go. Some countries arrange these things differently—but that's how it stands over here. If we can't charge a man we have to free him. . . ." Mayo's expression was cynical, resigned. " It won't be anything new—it often happens that the police know who committed a murder and yet are powerless to do anything about it. . . ."

" It's a pretty unsatisfactory state of affairs," Ashe said, thinking of Terry.

" Very," Mayo agreed, thinking of the law.

Ashe got to his feet. " Well, there it is—we'll have to wait and see, I suppose. . . . May I keep in touch, Inspector? "

" If you think it's worth your while," Mayo said. " In your place, I'd be thankful to drop the whole business."

The inspector's doubts about whether he would be able to bring the murder home to Terry turned out to be well founded. A week-end of intense activity by the police, Ashe learned on the Monday morning, had uncovered no new facts. Winter's house had been gone over a second time, with the greatest care, but the combing hadn't provided any material clues. Terry's cottage, and the ground around it, had been diligently searched, but nothing incriminating had been found. Of the rubber gloves that had been used, of the tool which had broken the lock, there was still no trace. The inspector's hope that someone might come forward—that someone might even have seen Terry on the move on the night of the murder—had proved a forlorn one. A final round of questioning by Mayo and his men had failed to extract any admissions from Terry, or catch him out in any contradictions. He'd simply stuck to his story—that he knew nothing about it.

On the Monday afternoon, therefore, what Mayo had foreseen came about. Terry was told that he could go. On the instructions of the police, and by arrangement with Laurence Winter, he returned to the cottage to stay there until the inquest was over. It was possible, Mayo said, that he might be charged later with attempting to stow away at Liverpool, but the decision on that would be taken elsewhere. Sheila MacLean was reported that evening to have visited him at the cottage and spent an hour or so with him. Ashe could see no point in attempting to renew contact with Terry himself, at least for the moment. He had no more questions to ask. He had tried out his " oddities " on Nancy, but she hadn't seemed very impressed, and he saw little prospect of getting anywhere with them. The whole affair seemed to have reached deadlock.

The inquest on Mavis Winter was held next day at Laybridge. There were no sensations. Inspector Mayo said that the police were still making inquiries, but significantly he didn't ask for an adjournment. Laurence Winter, pale and strained, was visibly holding himself in check and showed emotion only when the medical evidence referred to the violent pressure of two thumbs on either side of the victim's throat. The coroner took him gently through his account of the boat's stranding, of Mavis's departure, and of what he'd found at the house on his return. Mayo gave his reconstruction of what had probably happened. The jurymen all seemed quite satisfied and the verdict of murder by some person unknown followed automatically. Though Terry Booth's name had been on everyone's lips for days as the obvious suspect, he wasn't mentioned during the proceedings. The coroner happened to have strong views on not blackening a man if you couldn't charge him.

Ashe had a word or two with Laurence Winter after the verdict. Winter's main feeling now seemed to be thankfulness that the inquest was over and that the funeral could take place. He thought it an extra-ordinary thing that Mavis's murderer had apparently got away with it—Mayo had explained the position about Booth to him—but he wasn't really interested in revenge, which wouldn't bring Mavis back. All he could think of now, he said, was getting away. As soon as the funeral was over he'd probably put the house and garage up for sale, and later on take a flat in London for a while. He'd had enough of the country. . . . But for the moment he felt too tired to do anything. Ashe was sympathetic, and renewed his earlier offer of help if it should be required.

Outside the court Mayo was just getting into his car. Ashe went up to him.

" So it worked out just as you thought, Inspector."

Mayo nodded.

" What happens about Terry now?—is he really free, or are you still going to keep an eye on him? "

" Oh, he's free," Mayo said. " We haven't the men to spare for jobs like that. . . . I doubt if he will be for long, though."

" What do you mean? "

" He's been lucky, Mr. Ashe—but his luck won't last. He'll have a short run, you'll see. I know his type—they always take a crack at someone else, they can't help it. The leopard and his spots. . . . And the next time we'll get him. . . . The tragedy is that some other poor devil will probably have to suffer before we can deal with him."

" I still think you may be jumping to conclusions," Ashe said.

Grimly, Mayo shook his head. " I give him three months, Mr. Ashe—before he's up again somewhere for robbery with violence. Three months at the outside. . . . You mark my words! "

That afternoon there was an unexpected caller at the Ashe home. Ashe was standing by his car with a map, considering the best way to get to a rather cut-off farm he had to visit next day, when Sheila MacLean suddenly turned into the drive on her bicycle and dismounted beside him.

" Hullo, Sheila! " he said in a tone of surprise. The

girl had never been to the house before—Terry had always seemed to have plans of his own for her once they'd started courting—and Ashe still felt he scarcely knew her. As he looked at her, wondering why she'd come, he thought once again what an interesting and unusual face she had—a small, impassive oval, with green eyes set slightly on the slant.

" Could I see you and Mrs. Ashe for a minute? " Sheila said.

Ashe looked even more surprised at the oddly-phrased request. " Why, yes—if you want to. . . . Come along in." He led the way indoors. Nancy was just coming downstairs. " A visitor to see us," he called.

Nancy looked over the banisters, recognised the girl, and came slowly down. " Hullo . . ."

" Sheila wants to talk to us," Ashe said. He opened the sitting-room door and Sheila went in. Nancy, with a questioning lift of her eyebrows, followed.

The first few moments were awkward. Now that she was in the house Sheila appeared embarrassed and tongue-tied, and neither Ashe nor Nancy felt like asking her point-blank why she had come. On their side, too, conversation scarcely flowed. It was hard to know what to say to a girl whom they hardly knew, whose employer had just been strangled and whose boy friend was believed to be the murderer—especially as they didn't see eye to eye on the matter. Nancy said something rather vague about " this awful business " and how hard it must have been for Sheila, and waited for enlightenment.

It came at last. " Terry's gone," Sheila blurted out. " He went this afternoon. He's left the district."

Nancy showed no surprise. She felt like saying, " And a good thing, too! " but didn't.

Ashe said, " Do you know where he's gone? " He wasn't surprised, either.

Sheila shook her head. " He doesn't know himself yet. He said to some place where he wasn't known. . . . He's going to write to me as soon as he's settled."

" I see," Ashe said. There was a little silence.

" Mr. Winter doesn't want me any more," Sheila went on. " He says I'll have to leave at the end of the week."

Nancy gave an understanding nod. " He probably feels it isn't a very suitable arrangement," she said. " Being with you alone there all day."

" It isn't that. . . . He thinks I told Terry about the safe. He doesn't trust me any more."

Ashe frowned. " Did he say so? "

" No, but I can tell. . . . He didn't like me going on seeing Terry. . . . It was after that policeman talked to him again. . . ."

" You're probably imagining things," Ashe said.

" In any case," Nancy said, " Mr. Winter is planning to leave himself before long, so you couldn't have stayed. . . . And I'm sure you've nothing at all to worry about—you'll soon get another job."

" I won't," Sheila said. " Not for long. . . . I'm going to have a baby."

For a moment they both stared at her.

" Oh, *no*! " Ashe groaned. " For God's sake! "

Nancy said, " Are you sure? "

Sheila nodded. " It's two months. . . ."

" Terry's, I suppose? "

" Of course it's Terry's! " For the first time, Sheila's

shut-in face showed a flash of spirit. " It's no good blaming him, though—it was all my fault."

" Does Terry know? "

" Yes. . . . I told him just before I went home."

" Have you told your parents? "

" No." The wooden look was back.

" Have you told them about Terry at all? "

" No."

" You said you were going to."

" Well, I didn't."

Nancy sighed.

Ashe said, " But what happened when the police called on you? Didn't your parents want to know what it was all about? "

" They weren't in—they never knew. . . ." She suddenly seemed aware of Ashe's reproachful gaze. "I never wanted to go home in the first place," she burst out. " It was only Mr. Winter keeping on at me about it. . . ."

Nancy said, " Well, you'll have to tell them now— about the baby, I mean. You'll have to go back to them, Sheila."

" I'll *never* go back to them," Sheila said. " They wouldn't understand—especially about Terry. . . . Anyway, they wouldn't want me. They don't like me."

" Then what *are* you going to do? "

" I don't know. . . ." Sheila's mouth quivered. Two large tears gathered in her eyes and rolled slowly down her cheeks. She let them roll. Ashe thought she looked as though she'd had about as much as she could take.

" Have you any other relations you could go to? " Nancy asked.

Sheila shook her head. " Mrs. Dyson says I can't stay there, either."

" Because of the baby? "

" No—she doesn't know about that. . . . Because of me and Terry. . . . She says she's fed up with it all. . . ." Two more large tears coursed down Sheila's cheeks.

Ashe looked at Nancy questioningly. The girl, it was clear, needed help. They had a large house, plenty of room, there'd be no difficulty. . . . Nancy read the appeal in his face. For a moment she said nothing, as various practical considerations passed through her mind. She felt deeply sorry for the girl, but that wasn't everything. . . .

Finally, she compromised. " Well," she said, " you can stay here for a little while, Sheila, if you'd like to. I should expect you to help me, of course. . . . And it would only be temporary, just while we all decide what's best to be done."

Sheila dabbed her eyes with a squeezed-up handkerchief. " I *would* like to, Mrs. Ashe—I'll do anything you want me to. . . . And it won't be for long—only till Terry gets settled. He wants to marry me."

Nancy looked at her pityingly. Credulous girl!

" Anyway," she said, " would you want to marry him? After—all that's happened? "

" Yes, I would," Sheila said. " I'm sure he didn't do it. Just because he was in trouble before, they picked on him. Everyone's against him. It's not fair." Her lips tightened. " Anyone could have killed Mrs. Winter. Who's to say Mr. Winter didn't do it himself? "

" *Sheila!* " Nancy gazed at her in shocked anger. " That sort of talk isn't going to help Terry. . . ."

" Well, he might have done," Sheila said stubbornly. " They didn't really get on very well—they were always having arguments about money. . . . Nobody's bothered about him. Who's to say he didn't come home with Mrs. Winter that night? "

" Is this your own idea? " Nancy asked sharply.

Sheila hesitated. " Well, no—it's really Terry's. . . ."

" I thought as much! Sheila, can't you see he's just trying to shift the blame from himself, and doesn't care how he does it? He'd tell you anything. . . . It's wicked. . . . Mr. Winter tried his best to help him, all along. . . . Sheila, you're never to say anything like that again, anywhere."

Sheila's eyes dropped. She sat motionless, silent. She looked unutterably woebegone.

Nancy's anger faded. The girl, in her present state, could hardly be held accountable for what she said.

" All right, then, Sheila—you'd better bring your things over here to-morrow, and we'll see what can be done. . . ." Nancy turned to Ashe. " Do you think perhaps we ought to let Laurence know we're taking her, darling? "

" I suppose so," Ashe said. Rather thoughtfully, he went to the telephone.

It was Ashe's prison-visiting night, and soon after he'd rung Laurence Winter he drove off to keep his appointments. Usually he passed the journey mentally taking up the threads of his six cases, recalling where he'd left off last time and what he had to say and do.

But to-night he wasn't thinking about the prisoners. He was thinking once more about Terry—and not just what a damned young fool he'd been to get his girl into trouble and add to his problems. He was thinking about what Terry had said to Sheila—and Sheila to Terry—about Laurence. . . .

It was nonsense, of course. It couldn't for a moment be taken seriously. A bit of maid's gossip on Sheila's part, a reckless allegation on Terry's. . . . Carrying his campaign of spite a bit further. . . . A monstrous slander, actually—it wasn't surprising Nancy had gone off the deep end. . . . Not a thing to support it—and of course there wouldn't be. . . .

All the same, Ashe thought to himself, it *was* true that no one so far had thought of scrutinising Laurence's story about the various happenings. That was a simple fact. Everyone had been so sure Terry was the murderer—especially Mayo. The police had virtually concentrated on Terry. . . . No doubt it wouldn't have made the slightest difference—but surely someone should have checked on Laurence, if only as a matter of routine. . . .

Wryly, Ashe realised that he was now putting himself in much the same position as Terry and Sheila. . . . To give even a passing thought to a wild and slanderous accusation was almost as reprehensible as to make one. . . .

But then, if by some outside chance Terry *hadn't* killed Mavis—and those unexplained " oddities " were still in Ashe's mind—someone else must have done it. . . . And whoever one picked on as a possible suspect, the suspicion would probably seem pretty wild to start with. . . . So why boggle at Laurence?

Now, as he drove along, Ashe started to go over in his mind again all the things that were supposed to have happened during that fatal week-end. Just in an exploratory way—nothing more. After days of frustrating stalemate, he was in the mood to explore almost anything. . . . Re-examining the details. Testing Laurence's story in an impersonal way. . . . He recalled the facts of Mavis's return. He recalled Mayo's reconstruction, item by item. He recalled his own talk with Laurence at the house. He recalled the scene there— the things he'd been shown. The trail of damage, the picture, the safe, the broken lock, the path up the paddock. . . .

No, it all seemed to stand up very well. Just as one would expect it to. There were no inconsistencies. Nothing to make one wonder. Nothing at all peculiar.

At least, nothing much. . . .

Ashe frowned. There was one rather peculiar thing, perhaps. The state of the door. . . . It hadn't struck him at the time—but now that he came to think about it, it certainly was rather strange. . . .

He continued to think about it for the rest of the journey—and the more he dwelt on it, the stranger it seemed. . . .

The troubling fact lingered in the back of his mind all through the prison visit, came up for a fresh inspection on the way home, and gave him several wakeful hours that night. He still couldn't square it with reasonable probability. What was more, it no longer stood by itself. One thing had quickly led on to another. The seed of doubt, dropped in fertile soil, was growing well. . . . By morning, Ashe had decided that he must continue his exploration. Nancy wouldn't be very pleased, but that couldn't be helped.

He had his opportunity at the end of his morning round. Nancy had suggested that he should call at Mrs. Dyson's and pick up Sheila and her luggage, which he did. Sheila was in a much happier frame of mind now that her immediate future was settled, and sat beside Ashe with a look almost of contentment on her face. Ashe was beginning to think she was quite a girl. It was true she'd had her moments of tearful weakness the day before, but in general she seemed to have taken murder, and a suspect boy friend, and difficult parents, and now an incipient baby, very much in her stride. Behind that calm exterior, Ashe thought, there must be immense determination, tremendous guts—or else such a naïve detachment from the realities of the world that they simply passed her by. Ashe wasn't quite sure which—but he thought it was guts. Her devotion to Terry, her faith in him, had an iron quality—unless, of course, it was just stupidity. Again, Ashe wasn't sure. But she was certainly attached to him—remarkably so. Was it, Ashe wondered, because Sheila too had found herself a bit of a misfit, a bit of a reject from that harsh northern family, that she had so readily taken up with Terry in the first place? Was that the bond between them? It could be. . . .

Once they were on the road he abandoned his speculations and switched his mind to the practical questions he wanted to ask her. There wasn't going to be a lot of time so he waded right in.

" Sheila—you said yesterday that Mr. and Mrs.

P.F.—4

Winter had arguments about money.... I take it you overheard them."

"Yes," Sheila said. She looked surprised that he'd brought the subject up again—but she sounded quite co-operative. "I couldn't help it."

"Did you try?"

She glanced at him uncertainly—then smiled. "Not very hard."

"Well, that's honest. . . . I suppose Mr. Winter thought his wife spent too much?"

"Oh, no," Sheila said, "it wasn't that at all. . . . It was Mr. Winter trying to get money from Mrs. Winter."

Ashe turned sharply. "Really?"

"Yes, he was always asking her. . . . They were ever so rich, of course, but I think the money must all have been Mrs. Winter's, not his."

"H'm . . . What do you mean by 'always asking her'? How often did you hear him?"

"Well, two or three times. . . . Mrs. Winter was very stingy, she hated parting up. She used to send stale bread back to the shop and say she wouldn't pay for it."

"You don't mean it!"

"It's true. I know, because I had to take it. . . . She was always complaining about the prices of things and saying the bills weren't right—they didn't like her a bit at the shops."

"Did she and Mr. Winter ever *quarrel* about money?"

Sheila considered. "No, they didn't quarrel. I don't think Mr. Winter would have dared to quarrel."

"You mean Mrs. Winter wore the trousers?"

" She certainly did."

" So you never heard Mr. Winter speak angrily to her? "

" Oh, no—he always spoke softly and called her ' darling ' and fussed around her—but he often *looked* annoyed."

" Didn't you like Mrs. Winter? "

" Not very much."

" Then why did you stay with her? "

" Well, she never did *me* any harm."

Ashe concentrated on his driving for a moment, as they approached the main road into Springfield. Then he said, " It doesn't sound to me as though you'd a lot to go on when you said Mr. Winter might have killed his wife."

" I just don't think he liked her very much," Sheila said stubbornly.

Ashe grunted. " I suppose you discussed all this with Terry? "

" Well, yes. . . . *He* said he thought Mr. Winter must have done it, because there wasn't anyone else —and then I remembered how Mr. and Mrs. Winter had gone on together. . . ."

" M'm. . . ." They were approaching the drive now. " Well, I'm glad we've had this talk, Sheila—but it must be strictly between ourselves, you understand? You mustn't speak of it to anyone else. You know what gossips people are."

" Yes, I do. . . ." Sheila looked across at him hopefully. " Are you on Terry's side? "

" I don't know. . . . Oh, there is just one more thing. What's happened to the dog, Castor? Is he still in kennels? "

" He was yesterday."

Ashe nodded. " I thought he might be. . . . Well, here we are. . . ."

One advantage of having Sheila around became apparent that afternoon, when she took young Jane —who hadn't started school yet—for a walk. That left Nancy free for an hour, and gave Ashe a chance to tell her some of the things that had been passing through his mind.

" You know," he said, dropping down beside her on the settee, " I've been thinking about that night when Mavis Winter came back. . . . There's something I don't understand—something rather peculiar. . . ."

" What's that, darling? "

" *I* think it's peculiar, anyway. . . . Look—here was Mavis—a tiny, fragile woman. She kept a big boxer dog around. It always seemed to be her dog rather than Laurence's, and now there's no doubt it was— he hasn't even brought it home yet, though he's living on his own. . . . I had the impression it was a sort of guard dog. That suggests that Mavis was actually a rather nervous woman. . . . Yet what happened? Apparently she came back to spend a night by herself in a large, lonely house, without her dog—*and she didn't even bolt the back door before she went to bed.*"

" Oh . . . ? How do you know she didn't? "

" If she had, the bolts would have had to be forced as well as the lock. And they weren't. . . . Now doesn't that seem odd to you? "

Nancy considered. " Well, I don't think it's so very surprising," she said after a moment. " Lots of people would think locking the door was sufficient. . . . And

you can't say she was nervous just because she had a
boxer—some women like big dogs. You've often said
they get a kick out of it. . . ."

" Have I? . . ."

" Anyhow," Nancy said, " she obviously *wasn't* nervous—look at the way she came downstairs when she
heard the noise, and then chased whoever it was up
the paddock in her night-clothes. . . . If she could do
that, she certainly wasn't the kind of woman to bother
about bolting the door."

" *If* she could. . . ." Ashe said. " That's just it—can
you imagine it? Would *you* have done it? "

" I wouldn't, no. . . ." Nancy looked hard at him.
" What are you getting at? "

" Well," Ashe said, " I've been mulling over what
was supposed to have happened that night and I must
say I find some of it pretty difficult to believe. . . . I'm
just wondering if Mavis *did* come back alone after all.
Sheila's idea, in fact. . . . I know it sounds most un-
likely—but can we absolutely rule out the possibility
that Laurence came back with her? And killed her?
And then went back to the boat? . . . No one's checked
on it."

Nancy gazed at him in horror. " *Robert!* How can
you even say it! . . ."

" Why shouldn't I say it? I'm not making any
accusations—I'm being quite detached about it. I'm
just asking the question."

" But it's dreadful. . . . After all, Laurence is a sort
of friend."

" As far as I'm concerned, he's an acquaintance,"
Ashe said firmly. " A close acquaintance. I've always
got on with him quite well but I don't feel I owe him

any special loyalty. I don't really know him. . . . I certainly don't know him as well as I know Terry."

" As well as you thought you knew Terry, don't you mean? Honestly, Robert, you must be out of your mind—even to think of it. . . . *Why* would Laurence do a thing like that? What possible reason could he have? He and Mavis were very happy together. . . ."

" That's just it—were they? I'm not at all sure. . . . I've been having a talk with Sheila."

" *Robert!* Well, really—I think that's most unfair of you. . . . What on earth's the good of my ticking her off if you encourage her to tittle-tattle behind my back? "

" Sheila's a witness," Ashe said. " I had to ask her."

" A witness to what? "

" To the way Laurence and Mavis really got on. I'll tell you. . . ." Ashe repeated what Sheila had told him about the Winters' arguments over money, and how it was Laurence who'd approached Mavis each time, and how Mavis had seemed to run him. The story lost nothing in the telling. . . . Nancy listened stonily.

" Well, I don't think that amounts to much," she said, as he finished. " Most people argue about money —look at the way we go on sometimes. It doesn't mean we don't like each other."

" I don't come to you cap in hand," Ashe said. " You come to me. That's the normal set-up. Apparently the Winters' was different."

" So Sheila says. If you ask me, she's quite capable of making the whole story up. She's infatuated with Terry, she'd do anything to help him—and she's an

artful little thing. . . . I'm not at all sure we ought to
have let her come here. No wonder Laurence doesn't
trust her."

" You can't blame her for sticking by her boy
friend," Ashe said. "Especially now she's going to
have his child. . . . And you can't brush aside what
she said as easily as that, either. Some of the things
she told me square pretty well with what we knew of
Mavis ourselves. *You* said she was bossy—and she
must have had money before she met Laurence because
she told you she was travelling around the world for
years, and you can't do that on a shoestring. . . . If
you're detached about it, you must admit it *could* be
a classic situation."

" How do you mean? "

" Well, here's Laurence Winter, an attractive young
bachelor without any money. He meets a widow
fifteen years older than himself, and she has plenty. . . .
So he marries her."

" You're saying now he's a gigolo?"

" I'm not saying so, I don't know—but he could be.
I've seen him act rather like one, and so have you. . . .
Anyway, he marries this widow, thinking he'll be able
to get his hands on her money—and then she turns out
to be tight-fisted and dominating. All he can see ahead
is half a lifetime of reluctant hand-outs. But he knows
that once she's dead, he'll be in clover. . . . It's a classic
situation and a classic motive for murder."

" It's sheer imagination," Nancy said. " All you're
doing is supposing—you've absolutely nothing to go
on. . . . I don't know how you dare."

" I'm only considering the possibilities."

" Well, I don't think it's a possibility. It's fantastic.

. . . Good heavens, it would mean—it would mean that Laurence deliberately let Terry take the blame. . . . Worse than that—it would mean he arranged everything at the house, made it look like a breaking-in. . . . Faked everything. . . . Robert, you're crazy."

"What's crazy about it?" Ashe said. "I know it means all that—but if Laurence had had murder in mind, he'd have been practically forced to work things that way. Don't you see—without an alternative suspect, and a damn' good one, he'd have been number one suspect himself. He'd never have dared to do it. Having Terry around was just what he needed——" Ashe broke off, frowning. "In fact," he added, "he could have got Terry along in the first place *because* he wanted an alternative suspect. I never thought of that. . . ."

Nancy shook her head helplessly. "I wish you'd stop saying these terrible things. . . ."

"Well," Ashe said, "it *was* Laurence who took the initiative in getting hold of Terry, wasn't it? He rang the society and made the offer. . . . He even told them he didn't mind someone fairly tough!"

"Yes—but once he found out just how tough Terry was, you had a frightful job to persuade him. You know you did."

"He took him, though, didn't he? His reluctance could easily have been a pretence. He was in a buyer's market—he wasn't running any risks. He could see how anxious I was—he knew I'd go on pressing him. It was always open to him to agree in the end."

"Well, *I* think he agreed out of sheer kindness," Nancy said, "and you were ready enough to think so yourself at the time. It's horrible the way you've turned on him. . . . I think he's been marvellous all along—patient and understanding and really interested. . . . Look at the trouble he took over Terry. He did everything you wanted him to, and more. . . . Stamping the card, paying wages in advance, fixing him up in the cottage. . . ."

A slightly startled look crossed Ashe's face. "You know, that's another thing. . . . If Laurence had had the sort of plan we've been talking about, he'd have *had* to arrange that Terry would be living alone somewhere. Otherwise someone would have been able to say where he really was on the night of the murder."

"You're just forcing everything to fit," Nancy said. "Every little thing. . . . I suppose you'll be saying next that Laurence faked the office-breaking attempt as a build-up for what was coming."

"Well," Ashe said, "now that you mention it, he easily could have done. It would only have meant making a mark on the drawer and waiting till someone noticed it. He'd have known Terry would be angry and bitter about being suspected—just in the mood for breaking into the house and slashing the furniture. . . . The way things are, the whole affair could have been a deliberate frame-up from the beginning. Everything that happened could have been deliberate. Including running the boat aground—as an excuse to get Mavis back. *And* packing Sheila off to Northumberland for that week-end to get her out of the way. . . . You see, that's something else."

"If she had to go," Nancy said, "it was the obvious time."

"Yes, but *did* she have to go? She didn't want to. Laurence high-pressured her into it. . . . You can't say these things haven't any significance, when there are so many of them."

" They all seem to me to have quite an innocent, natural explanation," Nancy said. " You keep looking for the other sort. . . . Honestly, Robert, I think what you've been saying is absolute nonsense. You wouldn't even have thought of Laurence if Terry hadn't put the idea into your head. And he's a tainted source, if ever there was one."

" It isn't important where the idea came from," Ashe said. " All that matters is whether there's anything in it."

" Well, I'm quite sure Laurence would never have done anything of the sort. He's much too nice."

" You mean he *seems* nice—and I agree. But if he was actually a cunning crook who'd married a widow for her money, you'd expect him to seem nice, wouldn't you. The part would call for it. . . . And if he wasn't capable of playing the part, he'd never have gone into the business in the first place. If he'd had shifty eyes and a pock-marked face he'd have chosen something else. Charm's the first essential for a gigolo."

Nancy stirred impatiently. " Well, you can say what you like, but I'm positive Laurence didn't kill Mavis. . . . What's more, I agree with Inspector Mayo—I think Terry did it. Everything points to him."

" Everything would point to him if there was a frame-up," Ashe said.

Nancy shook her head. " No one could frame Terry's nature—he just is that sort of man. He's vicious and brutal and he doesn't give a damn about anyone except himself. Every single thing he does is in character. Look how he's got Sheila into trouble. . . ."

"For heaven's sake, that could happen to anyone. . . . It doesn't mean he's a murderer."

"It doesn't increase one's faith in him, does it? And now he's gone off into the blue. I don't suppose she'll ever hear from him again—though it's probably just as well."

"If he was going to clear off for good," Ashe said, "why would he have bothered to try and convince her he was innocent? Why would he have bothered to put up this Winter idea?"

"Liars don't have to have good reasons. . . . What about that prisoner you told me about—Hawkins, wasn't it? What was the purpose of his lie—where did it get him? These people just can't help it."

Ashe said nothing. Hawkins was a sore point with him. Right at the beginning of his prison visiting, in his very green days, the man had so convinced him he was incapable of committing the offence he was in jail for that Ashe had gone to the governor about it, with a wonderful theory to explain a possible miscarriage of justice. And the governor had produced Hawkins's record, which had shown that he'd committed the same offence eleven times before. . . .

"Really, darling," Nancy went on, "I think you ought to forget about Terry—and the whole business. You know it's only because of Terry that you've thought up all these things about Laurence. It isn't healthy—you're getting everything out of proportion. You're letting yourself be carried away. And it's all so silly. . . . It's not even as though you really like Terry very much. . . ."

"I wouldn't say that. . . ."

" Well, you're certainly not fond of him, he's not a close friend of yours. How could he be?—you've nothing whatever in common. . . . When things seemed to be going all right with him, you almost forgot about him—you hardly saw him at all. . . ."

" It wasn't necessary."

" Exactly. . . . But now you're starting all over again. Robert, it's a sort of pride with you, don't you see— you don't want to admit that your judgment about him was wrong. . . . Darling, I do understand and it's terribly natural—he did seem to be a sort of achievement, and you rather fancied yourself as a father-figure. . . . But it didn't work out, and it's no good being stubborn about it now, and getting het up, and inventing these perfectly preposterous theories when you must know there's nothing in them. . . . Terry isn't the only person in the world—other people have rights too. This idea about Laurence—it would be too awful if it got around. . . . It isn't even as though Terry's in any danger. . . . He's been released—his life's not at stake. . . ."

" In a sense," Ashe said, " his life's at stake almost as much as though he still risked being hanged. If he killed Mavis—well, then he's hopeless, worthless, and it doesn't matter. I'd write him off without another thought. . . . But if he didn't, and he's been wrongly suspected, he'll be so full of hate and resentment he'll go to the devil when he needn't have done. . . . That's the thought I can't bear. . . . Maybe there is some pride in it—maybe I did think I'd done a good job on him, and can't believe I've failed. . . . Well, what's wrong with that? I *don't* believe it, and I won't until I have to. There's an outside chance he's innocent,

and if he is, he needs help. He's getting some from
Sheila—she may be the one thing that's holding him
together—but it's not enough. I feel I've got to do
what I can. . . ."

Nancy gazed at him, disapproving and yet admiring.
" Darling, you're so credulous sometimes. . . . Anyway,
what *can* you do? "

" I'm going down to that boat place," Ashe said,
" to see what Laurence actually was doing that week-
end. . . . I know I've very little to go on, and I'm
certainly not accusing him. . . . I'm probably nuts!
All the same, I'm going to make sure about him—one
way or the other."

III

ASHE REARRANGED two professional appointments that he'd made for the following day—not without causing some inconvenience to clients—and immediately after surgery next morning he set off in his car for the Essex coast, some three hours' drive away. He'd equipped himself with a large-scale map of the district, and Sheila had been able to give him enough information for him to start his inquiries. Mr. Winter's boat, she'd said, was called *Dolphin*, and there was a boatman at Salfleet named Ted Pettit, who kept an eye on it. Ashe thought he'd go straight to Pettit. Nancy—very much against the trip but realising that she couldn't stop it—had urged him at least to be discreet in his questioning, and he'd promised to be careful. He would pretend, he'd decided, that he was thinking of buying a boat himself, and gradually work round to the subject of the murder week-end without making his interest too obvious. It would be a bit tricky, but Ashe was used by now to conducting delicate interviews and he felt quite confident.

Salfleet, he discovered on arrival, was a very small place indeed. There was a row of about six cottages, a tiny general shop in someone's front parlour, a petrol pump for the boats, a telephone kiosk, and—a little away from the rest—a very modest pub. They were all ranged along a quarter of a mile of poorly-made-up

road that lay immediately beneath a low sea-wall.
Ashe parked his car and climbed the wall for a better
look round.

The view on the seaward side was fascinating.
Stretching away, apparently for miles, was a maze of
shining creeks and rills, winding between grey-green
saltings and steep banks of mud. There appeared to
be one main channel, some distance from the wall,
where quite a lot of small craft were lying placidly
at moorings. They were too far away for Ashe to read
their names, but *Dolphin* was presumably one of them.
There was no sign of any activity on the boats—the
whole seaward side of the wall seemed quite deserted.
Because the day was fine and sunny, everything looked
most attractive, but in less good conditions it would
obviously be a bleak and desolate place.

For a moment or two Ashe studied his map, identify-
ing the various channels and seeing where they led.
Then he returned to the car and drove to the little
shop to inquire for Ted Pettit. The boatman, he was
told, would be found in a houseboat dried out at the
edge of the saltings some way beyond the pub. He
drove on, past a line of small rowing boats and tenders
drawn up on a grassy verge at the head of the creek.
He could see the houseboat now. He continued on past
the pub, past a parked car—and suddenly checked
in astonishment. A familiar figure was just getting out
of the car. It was Inspector Mayo!

Ashe pulled up and walked back to join him. Mayo
appeared to be on his own. " Well—*hullo*, Inspector,"
he said.

" Why, Mr. Ashe! " Mayo looked astonished, too—
and not particularly pleased.

"You're about the last person I expected to see," Ashe said. "What brings you here?"

"Oh—business."

"H'm. . . . You wouldn't be reopening the Winter case, would you?"

"The case was never closed," Mayo said shortly.

"Because you couldn't prove the murder was done by Terry?"

"Well, there was a bit of ground we still had to cover. . . ." Mayo looked faintly embarrassed. "Just a few routine inquiries."

"About Laurence Winter?"

"Just a check."

"That's most interesting," Ashe said. "As a matter of fact, I've been wondering about Winter too—it may be that we've been thinking along the same lines. . . ." He paused. "Perhaps you would tell me one thing, Inspector. Did Mavis Winter have much money to leave?"

Mayo hesitated. "Actually, she did. . . . Quite a bit."

"How much?"

"Well, it'll be in the papers any day now so I suppose there's no harm in telling you. . . . I gather she was worth about a hundred and seventy thousand pounds when she died."

Ashe stared at him. "Good God!"

"It seems her first husband was a wealthy business-man, and she inherited it from him."

"And does Winter get it now?" Ashe asked, in rising excitement.

"I understand the bulk of it was willed to him, yes. Mrs. Winter had no near relatives. . . . But if you're

thinking what I think you are, Mr. Ashe, the set-up
isn't all that unusual. A man can inherit a fortune
without being a murderer."

" Still, you obviously think there's something to be
inquired into," Ashe said, "or you wouldn't be here.
. . . And so do I. . . . Look, Inspector, I've been
thinking a lot about Winter—I'd like to tell you . . ."

" Well . . . ? "

Bluntly, Ashe outlined his frame-up idea, bringing
out all the points in its favour as they'd emerged from
his talk with Nancy. Mayo listened with rather
reluctant interest to the reconstruction.

" H'm—bit far-fetched, isn't it? " he commented,
as Ashe finished.

" If Terry didn't do it, the truth's bound to be far-
fetched," Ashe said. " Anyway, I thought it was just
possible Winter went back with his wife that Monday
evening—so I decided to try and check on his move-
ments. . . . Surely that's why you're here, too? "

Mayo didn't deny it. " A purely routine check," he
said again. " I certainly don't expect anything to
come of it. . . . In my experience, Mr. Ashe, most
crimes of violence are sordid and obvious, not clever
and imaginative."

" Perhaps the imaginative criminals don't get
caught," Ashe said.

Mayo smiled grimly. " I doubt if that's the explanation. . . ." He was silent for a moment. " I
suppose it hasn't occurred to you," he said, " that if
Winter had wanted to frame Booth for the murder
of his wife, he could easily have planted something of
Booth's in the house—made it appear that he'd dropped
something. Then Booth would almost certainly have

been convicted and hanged. As it is, there's no more than a grave suspicion. . . . Why would Winter only have done half a job? "

" Perhaps the complete job seemed too risky," Ashe said. " Winter would have had to leave some loophole, wouldn't he, in case by some unforeseen chance Terry turned out to have an alibi for that night. . . . I mean, if something of Terry's had been found in the house, and it was proved afterwards that he'd spent the night dead drunk in a police cell in Camden Town, that would have shown there'd been a frame-up, and Winter would have been in trouble at once."

Mayo gave a rather grudging nod. " Yes, that's a point," he said. He started, not very decisively, to move off.

Ashe moved with him, step for step. " Anyway," he said, " wouldn't it be a good thing if I tagged along with you while you make your inquiries? I was going to talk to the boatman, Ted Pettit—I suppose you were, too, he seems the obvious chap—but I don't want to queer your pitch."

" Very thoughtful of you! " Mayo said. " All right, you can come along. . . . But for goodness' sake don't start making any accusations."

" I won't," Ashe said. " I'll leave it entirely to you."

They found Ted Pettit outside the houseboat, varnishing a mast laid on trestles. He was a man of about thirty, tall and slim, with frank blue eyes and a lean, tanned face. A battered old naval cap, worn slightly askew, gave him a cheerful, insouciant air.

Judging by the signs of work in progress around the place, he was much more than a boat-minder—it looked as though he had quite a prosperous one-man repair business.

Mayo introduced himself—but not Ashe. " I'm making a few inquiries in connection with the death of Mrs. Mavis Winter," he began rather formally.

" Oh, yes . . . " Pettit said.

" You knew her, of course ? "

" Yes—quite well. She often used to come down with Mr. Winter. . . . I could hardly believe it when I read she'd been murdered."

" You look after Mr. Winter's boat, I'm told."

" That's right—the *Dolphin*." Ted pointed out over the creek. " That's her—the white cruiser astern of the blue sloop."

Mayo nodded. " I'm interested in what happened down here during the week-end of the murder," he said, " and I think it's possible you may be able to help me. . . ." He glanced up at the houseboat. It had electric light and the telephone connected. Some of the windows were curtained, others weren't. " You live here, do you? "

" Yes, at the far end. This end's the workshop."

" Do you live alone? "

Ted grinned. " So far."

" Well, if you're here all the time I imagine you must see practically everything that goes on. Good place for keeping your eye on things, eh? "

" Yes, it's as good a spot as any for watching the creek. . . . And you have to, round here, I can tell you."

" Really? "

" Yes—several times we've had young hooligans interfering with the boats."

" H'm—that's a problem everywhere these days. . . . Well, now, I'd like you to think back to that Saturday afternoon before the tragedy. Mr. and Mrs. Winter arrived by car, I believe."

" That's right," Ted said. " About three o'clock."

" Did they both seem in good spirits? "

" Yes, fine. . . . They always were when they were down here."

" Mr. Winter wasn't—well, specially quiet—anything like that? "

" No—just ordinary."

" Did they say how long they were going to stay? "

Ted thought for a moment. " Yes, they said till the Wednesday."

" I see. . . . And what did they do when they got here? "

" Well—Mr. Winter and I had a little chat about the boat—his dynamo hadn't been charging properly and he wanted me to see if it needed a new belt. . . . Then they went out in their dinghy to *Dolphin* and after about an hour they steamed off."

" Where would they have gone to—any idea? "

" Oh, just around the creeks—maybe out a little way. . . . There's miles of sheltered water round here, you can cruise for days. . . . Mr. Winter knows the place very well—he's done a lot of pottering around."

" Aha. . . . So when did you see them again? "

" On the Monday afternoon. They came ashore with a couple of cans to get some more petrol and do a bit of shopping. Then they went off again and I didn't see them any more until Mr. Winter came and told me *Dolphin* was aground. That was on the Monday evening. . . ."

" Oh, so you knew about the grounding at the time? "

" Knew about it—I'll say! I helped to get her off."

" I see. . . . Perhaps you'd tell me exactly what happened that evening—from the beginning."

" Well, it was just after dark when I heard Mr. Winter at his car——"

Mayo interrupted. " Where had he left his car? "

" Over there by the dinghies. . . . He was telling Mrs. Winter to be careful how she drove. Then the car went off, and Mr. Winter came along here, pretty fed up. He said *Dolphin* had run aground on a mud bank and was lying on her ear and that he'd need my help to get her off."

" Did he say anything about his wife? "

" He said she hadn't fancied a night aboard at that angle and had gone home. . . ."

Ashe, who'd been following the inspector's very thorough catechism with approval, suddenly said, " Do boats often run aground here? "

Ted grinned. " You bet they do—there's someone high and dry most week-ends. If you move around on a falling tide you're bound to touch the putty sooner or later. . . ."

" Even if you're very skilful? "

" Oh, it could happen to anyone."

" *Is* Mr. Winter skilful? "

" He isn't bad—not for a water motorist! I like a bit of sail myself. . . ."

Mayo gave Ashe a slightly sardonic glance and

turned to Ted again. " Right, go on—what happened about *Dolphin*? "

" Well, there wasn't any hurry, because the tide was still falling and there was nothing we could do for hours. So we went into the pub and had a few beers. We were there till nearly ten, and then we rowed out to the boat. . . ."

" Did Mr. Winter seem at all agitated? "

" Well, he was a bit worried, and when we got to *Dolphin* I could see why. . . . The boat was leaning the wrong way, down the slope instead of up it, and he was afraid she might fill when the tide rose. . . . As a matter of fact he was lucky, because on the other side of the channel the mud's almost vertical and if she'd grounded there she might have fallen over and been a total loss. . . . Anyway, we took various precautions, and then we had some more beer and waited for the tide to rise. We had quite a job with the boat, getting her floating again in the dark, and we were both pretty worn out when it was all over. That was well after midnight. So we dossed down in the saloon. In the morning Mr. Winter got breakfast and I squared up on deck and about ten we went ashore. Mr. Winter tried to phone his wife to tell her the boat was all right, but he couldn't get any reply, and as it was another fine day he said he thought he'd go off cruising again—and he did."

" So in fact," Mayo said, " Mr. Winter was with you all the time between, say, eight o'clock on the Monday evening and about half past ten on the Tuesday morning."

" That's right," Ted said.

" And when did he go home—do you know? "

" On the Wednesday morning. I drove him to the station as he didn't have his car, and he caught the eleven-thirty-two."

Mayo gave a satisfied nod. " Well, you've been most helpful, Ted—I think that's about all. . . . By the way, don't mention this conversation to anyone— it's just been a routine inquiry and I don't want people getting wrong ideas. Understand? "

" Sure," Ted said. " Glad I was able to help. . . ." He picked up his brush and went to work again on the spar.

Mayo started to walk briskly away. In silence, Ashe accompanied him. The inspector was looking much better tempered now—and the reason was only too plain. Assuming Ted was telling the truth— and Ashe had never met a more patently honest man— Winter had a complete alibi for the Monday night.

Surprisingly, as they approached the pub, Mayo said, " Let's have a drink."

Ashe was in no mood for a celebration—but he soon discovered that that wasn't the purpose. Over two half-pints, Mayo quickly and skilfully confirmed with the landlord the basic points in Ted's story. Ted and Mr. Winter had been in the pub from eight until nearly ten on the Monday night, the landlord had heard all about the grounding and what they were going to do about it, and on the Tuesday morning he'd seen them rowing ashore from *Dolphin* and he'd gone out and had another talk with them. . . . Even when convinced, Ashe thought, the inspector was thorough.

" Well," Mayo said, as they left the pub, " that seems to take care of Winter, doesn't it. . . . So much for theories, Mr. Ashe ! "

Ashe was less easily satisfied. Still in the forefront
of his mind was that startling disclosure about the
money. It had worked in with his theory so perfectly
—it had seemed to confirm all his latent suspicions.
Now, faced with an impasse, he started to look for a
way round. And, very soon, he found one.

"I agree that Winter has got a cast-iron alibi for
the Monday night," he said, "but he doesn't seem to
have one for the Tuesday—he was away on his own,
in the boat. He could have landed somewhere that
day, somewhere quiet, and made his way home, and
killed his wife on the Tuesday night. . . . That would
fit in well with other things, too. I've always thought
it a bit surprising that the contractor fellow who
limed the paddock on the Tuesday didn't notice
anything amiss—but if nothing had happened by
then, he wouldn't have. . . . I realise the medical
evidence is a bit of a snag, but they're often wrong
about the time of death."

"They weren't wrong this time," Mayo said. "Mrs.
Winter was definitely murdered on the Monday night."

"Can you really be so certain?"

"I can be positive," Mayo said, "and I'll tell you
why."

"Well?"

"When you called on Winter that day, after the
murder, did you see the place where the body was
found?"

"Not close to, no."

"Well, as I told you, it was in the long grass at the
side—you'll probably remember there's a strip there,
to the right of the path, that's got rather out of hand.
Some of the lime from the blower had blown over the

edge of the paddock proper and dusted this strip
thinly but pretty evenly to a depth of about fifteen
feet. The body was lying nine feet inside the outer
edge of the dusted area."

" Well? " Ashe said again, puzzled.

" Well, Mr. Ashe, the liming was done between
ten and eleven o'clock on the Tuesday morning. I
checked the time with the contractor—his name's
John Cole—and he says he was through by eleven. . . .
There was lime dust on top of the body—but none
underneath. Not a trace. Which means that Mavis
Winter was lying there dead in the grass between ten
and eleven on the Tuesday morning when the dusting
was done. At half past ten that morning Laurence
Winter was still here—and he'd been here all the
week-end. So he couldn't have killed her. It's conclusive."

Ashe drove home in a deflated and self-critical mood.
Now that his idea about Winter had been exploded,
he could have kicked himself for ever having entertained it. Nancy had been so right—he *had* let himself
be carried away. As he did only too often. Turning a
blind eye to anything that didn't suit him. Wishful
thinking. . . . *Of course* Laurence hadn't done it. There
never had been anything against him, really. Very
much on the contrary. His kindly actions over Terry
had seemed sinister only because Ashe had twisted
them, putting the worst possible construction on
everything. Sheila had no doubt exaggerated about
the domestic set-up—and Ashe had made fanciful
additions. After all, a young man with an older,
well-to-do wife was bound to appear a bit of a gigolo

at times. Laurence's dazed distress after Mavis's death had obviously been genuine. . . . Ashe felt now, as Nancy had done all along, that his suspicions had been shameful. Wanting to help Terry wasn't a sufficient reason for trying to shift the blame to Laurence.

Ruefully, when he got back, he told Nancy of his dramatic but abortive day. " It seemed to start so well," he said. " When I heard about that money I could have sworn I was on the right track. . . . A hundred and seventy thousand pounds—just think of it ! "

" It is rather staggering," Nancy agreed. " I'd never have guessed she was as rich as that."

" It looked an absolute cinch for a motive. . . . And then—complete collapse. An alibi to end all alibis. . . . I could have crawled into the ground when Mayo told me about the lime."

" Well, if you ask me," Nancy said, " it's a very good thing Laurence *has* got an alibi. . . . Otherwise you'd almost certainly have gone on suspecting him— and it really was quite ridiculous. . . ."

Ashe nodded slowly.

" Mind you," he said, " I wasn't the only one— Mayo thought it was worth looking into as well. . . . It may have been routine, but *he* obviously didn't think Laurence was above suspicion—not at first."

" He's a policeman, darling—it's his job to be suspicious."

Ashe grunted.

" Anyhow," Nancy said, " you seem to be back with Terry as the only suspect. Do you still think he didn't do it ? "

Ashe gave a dejected shrug. " *I* don't know. . . . I don't know what to think. . . ."

As it happened, he had little chance to think about anything except his work during the next twenty-four hours. Jobs had been accumulating in his absence and he spent the evening catching up with some of them. The next morning's surgery proved to be unusually heavy, and at midday he was called out urgently by one of his best clients to attend the premature foaling of a valuable mare. It was a case that required all his professional skill, and for some hours he was entirely absorbed.

He got back home at half past six—tired, but well satisfied with his efforts. Nancy, he gathered, was having a bath. Sheila had been helping to put the children to bed, and was now tidying up in the kitchen. In her unobtrusive way, Ashe thought, she was really very capable about the house—as well as pleasant to look at. He poured himself a glass of beer and sat down on a kitchen chair to drink it.

" I had a letter from Terry to-day," Sheila said.

" *Did* you? " Ashe looked interested.

" Yes—Mr. Winter sent it round."

" Well — good for Terry! How's he getting on? "

" Would you like to read it? "

" I would, yes," Ashe said, " if you're sure you don't mind. . . ."

Sheila produced the letter from her handbag. The envelope was dirty and a bit crumpled. Ashe was able to make out the word " Essex " on the postmark, but the rest was indecipherable. He took out the single, folded sheet of exercise-book paper and quickly ran his eye down it.

The letter said, in part:

I got a job, clearing a building sight near Chelmsford. Its labourers work and a lousy job really not much pay but the best I could get without a caracter. They dont know anything about me here so theres no trouble about that. Its good not to have people staring at you all the time thinking your a killer. Any rate I'll do better soon I got some plans you can be sure. I'll beat the lot of them you'll see. Nobodys going to keep me down. Dont you worry I'll get hold of some money before long, then we'll get married. Look after young Terry wont you. . . .

The letter ended affectionately. There was no address.

Ashe read it through again before handing it back. " Well, it sounds all right," he said.

He took his beer into the sitting-room. In a few moments Nancy joined him there.

" Hullo, darling—I thought I heard you come in. . . . How did it go? "

" Not so bad," Ashe said. " Mother and daughter are both doing well. . . ."

" That's wonderful."

" Hamilton's delighted—says I'm the best vet in the county."

" Of course you are. . . . Was it very tricky? "

" The first four hours were the worst."

" Poor old thing—you must be worn out."

" I'll be all right after I've freshened up." Ashe

felt for his pipe, took it out of his pocket, put it back again. " So it seems you were wrong about Terry. . . . He hasn't abandoned Sheila."

" Oh, she's told you? "

" She showed me the letter."

Nancy nodded. " She showed it to me, too. . . . Yes, I do seem to have been wrong—about that."

" I was rather struck by the letter," Ashe said. " He's obviously fighting back, not giving in."

" It seemed a bit boastful to me," Nancy said.

" I'd call it spirited."

Nancy smiled. " I'm sure you would! I'm just wondering *how* he plans to get hold of the money he talks about."

" Get a better job—work for it. . . ."

" Let's hope you're right," Nancy said.

" I suppose you think he's plotting another crime? "

" It wouldn't surprise me at all."

" At least you must admit that he seems fond of Sheila."

" That doesn't mean much. . . . Murderers can be as fond of their girls as anyone else, I suppose."

" He can't do anything right for you, can he? " Ashe said. " You were against him because you thought he was going to leave Sheila in the lurch—and now he rallies round you're still against him. . . . *Women!* "

He finished his beer at a gulp and went off upstairs.

Sitting alone in his study later that evening, Ashe found himself thinking again about the letter, going over its phrases. . . .

Since his return from Salfleet, he'd been very near to admitting in his own mind the likelihood that Terry had, after all, committed the murder. With Laurence in the clear, it had seemed impossible to avoid the conclusion. But now this letter had suddenly brought all Ashe's doubts flooding back. He could be wrong, of course—he was a partisan and an eager one—but it hadn't *sounded* to him like the letter of a man with a brutal murder on his mind. Whatever Nancy might say, it had seemed to fit the picture of a struggling, basically decent Terry much better than of an incorrigible young thug trying to throw dust in his girl's eyes. That letter, surely, was the work of an innocent man. . . .

At once, Ashe was back in the toils again. If Terry was innocent, who was guilty? If Terry hadn't done it, and Laurence was ruled out, who was left? No one. . . . No one, at least, with all the knowledge the murderer would have needed—or with any discernible motive for doing what had been done, in the way it had been done. Malice, or a carefully-plotted frame-up, both made sense. Nothing else did. The choice still seemed to lie between the two men. . . .

Ashe's thoughts swung back to Winter. To his strong, his immensely-strong, motive. . . . He'd certainly been lucky to have that alibi. *Damned* lucky. Almost incredibly so, when you came to think of the chances. . . . To *happen* to run aground, to *happen* to have Ted Pettit with him for every moment of those vital hours, to *happen* to have arranged for his paddock to be dusted just when proof of the time of death was most needed. . . . Things couldn't have worked out more conveniently for him if the whole sequence of events had been deliberately planned. . . .

The incredulous feeling stayed with Ashe. The alibi

was too pat, too perfect. In his chagrin over Mayo's revelation, he hadn't thought of it at the time—but now he did. It was like a road block thrown up against attack. An impregnable one, too. Solid—nothing phoney about it. A genuine alibi. There was no doubt about it—Laurence *hadn't* killed Mavis. No one could be in two places at once. And yet, somehow, the alibi reeked of forethought. . . . But why in heaven's name would anyone organise an alibi for a crime he wasn't going to commit?

Even as Ashe posed the question, a possible answer leapt to his mind.

A man might well want an alibi for a crime he knew he'd be suspected of—a crime he'd arranged for some-one else to commit!

It was an intriguing idea. Fanciful, of course, even by Ashe's standards. But it answered the question, and he let his mind play with it. Theoretically, Laurence *could* have got someone else to do the job for him. A hired assassin. . . . Such things still happened. For a whacking consideration, a large cut of that hundred and seventy thousand pounds, he might have persuaded someone. Someone who had no connection with Mavis, who wasn't likely to be suspected. . . . And he'd have remained secure himself behind his alibi.

But who? Supposing it had happened—which wasn't likely—where could such a man be looked for now? The field was wide open. . . .

Or *was* it?

Ashe frowned. He was thinking again of the alibi that would have been so necessary to Winter. The dusting, that had fixed the time. . . . Laurence surely wouldn't have dared to take any chances over that. It was crucial. He'd have had to *know* that the dusting would be done in his absence, and done properly, and at the right time, and that nothing whatever would be allowed to stand in its way. He'd have had to be able to rely absolutely on the man who did it. . . . And who could he have relied on to that extent except the hired assassin himself—the man he was paying to do the job for him, whose own neck would be at stake?

It was fantastically improbable, of course—but suppose it was the contractor, John Cole, who had come to the house that Monday night and strangled Mavis?

The ringing of the telephone broke into his thoughts. Still preoccupied, he went into the hall to answer it. The voice at the other end gave him a shock. It was Laurence Winter on the line.

" Hullo, Robert," Winter said. " Look—something rather disturbing has come up. . . . I can't talk about it on the phone—but I'd very much like to have a private word with you, if you're not tied up."

" No, I'm free. . . ." Ashe had to make a conscious effort to sound normal—it wasn't easy to talk with ordinary friendliness to a man you'd just been thinking of as a potential villain. " Come over by all means."

" That's just it, I'm afraid I can't," Winter said. " I'm stuck here waiting for someone to ring me. . . . I wondered if you could possibly drive over? Don't trouble if it isn't convenient—but I would very much like to see you. . . ."

Ashe hesitated. " Well, I have had quite a day. . . ."

Then curiosity got the better of him. " All right," he said, " I'll be along in about fifteen minutes."

" Good man! I'll be seeing you." The telephone clicked.

Ashe went in to tell Nancy. She looked a bit surprised. " I wonder what it can be. . . . Anyway, you'll try not to be too late, won't you? "

" I certainly will. . . . I told him I'd had a big day."

Ashe picked up a torch and went out rather thoughtfully to the garage. Already he was beginning to wish he'd said " No " instead of " Yes. " In his present frame of mind, the meeting was bound to be a strain, an embarrassment. He was in a most equivocal position. . . .

It wasn't until he was approaching Winter's house that he felt the first twinge of apprehension. How much did Laurence know, he wondered, about his recent activities? Could he have learned about that visit to Salfleet? Could he have guessed what had been passing through his mind lately? It was a bit odd, the way he'd practically insisted that Ashe should visit *him*. . . . Suppose Laurence *was* a murderer. . . . It was absurdly melodramatic—but might this be some sort of trap? Ashe's uneasiness increased as he left his car and started to walk down the long, quiet path to the house. The place was so cut off, so very silent. And there had been one murder there already. . . . Then he took a grip on himself. It was idiotic to let his imagination run away with him like that. Apart from anything else, Laurence would guess that he'd told Nancy where he was going. He'd never dare to do anything. . . . All the same, Ashe's pulse beat a little faster than usual as Winter came to the door.

Once he was inside the lighted hall, he felt ashamed of his fears. Winter's greeting was friendly and natural —and very grateful. " I'm so sorry I had to bring you out," he said, " but I couldn't leave—I'm trying to get hold of my solicitor. He's at some function and he'll be ringing me directly he gets home. . . . Would you care for a drink? "

" I don't think so, thanks," Ashe said. He went ahead into the sitting-room and took the chair Winter indicated. " What's on your mind, Laurence? "

Winter sat down opposite him. " You'll be surprised. . . . I had an anonymous letter by the evening post, accusing me of murdering my wife ! "

Ashe stared at him. " Good God ! " He didn't have to pretend he was startled.

" I rather think it's from Booth, but I'm not certain —that's why I wanted to see you. I thought you'd probably know his handwriting."

Ashe took the letter from him. He saw at once that it was from Terry. It was a short note, but very much to the point. It said :

I know you killed your wife you rotten lousy bastard. You was always trying to get dough out of her when she was alive now you reckon you got the lot, well, you wont get away with it. She wouldnt of come back alone that night she never done it before. I bet you come back with her. You think your bloody smart but your wrong they'll hang you.

For a moment Ashe sat in silence. His face was strained—from now on this interview was going to be even more difficult than he'd feared. He was reluctant to look up, to meet Laurence's eyes. He had to force himself to. "Yes, it's from Booth," he said. "Not very pleasant. . . . I'm sorry."

Winter shrugged. "It's unpleasant, but it's exactly what I'd have expected of him. Reckless, abusive, moronic. . . . Extraordinary he should think he can help himself in this way. . . . He's a real bad hat, Robert, the worst I ever came across. . . ."

"You take it very well," Ashe said. "In your place I'd be hitting the ceiling."

Winter gave a twisted smile. "My dear chap, he murdered my wife, he's done all the harm he can do to me—why should I get worked up about a letter? He's a horrible creature, and one day he'll get his deserts. . . . No, what I find more upsetting is the way Sheila MacLean has obviously been talking to him. Most of the letter's pure rubbish, of course, but it is true that Mavis never spent a night here alone before, she never needed to—and Booth wouldn't have known that if Sheila hadn't told him. . . . It's an odd thing— we always treated her well, we did a great deal for her —yet she must dislike me intensely, or she wouldn't be helping Booth with this scurrilous nonsense. . . . It's rather depressing. . . ."

"She's had a lot of trouble," Ashe said. "I think one has to make allowances."

Winter shook his head. "I've made all the allowances I can. I'm not at all sure she wasn't working in with Booth from the beginning—that's why I felt in the end I had to get rid of her. . . . Frankly, I was a bit surprised when you took her on—in the circumstances. . . ."

"We didn't have a lot of choice," Ashe said. "She came round in a pretty bad state. . . . I didn't tell you at the time, but everyone will know soon—the fact is, she's pregnant by Booth. She didn't know where to turn. We couldn't show her the door."

" Good lord! " Slowly, Winter's clouded expression cleared. " I *see*! Well, that explains it. . . . I confess it struck me as a rather unfriendly act at the time—a bit of a blow in the face. . . . Now I understand. . . . What's she going to do, Robert? "

" Marry him, she says."

" God, what a fate! Still, if they're birds of a feather . . . I don't know, I can't make up my mind about her. . . . I must say I'll be glad when I'm out of it all."

" I'm sure you will. . . . How are your plans going? "

" Oh, I've seen the auctioneers—I'm selling everything. What else can I do? This place gives me the horrors now. . . . It's the same with the boat—I'll never go near it again. . . . I'm going to try and make a clean break with the past—it's the only way. . . ."

Ashe nodded. " I do understand—I'm sure I'd feel the same. . . ." He got to his feet. " What are you going to do about the letter? "

Winter gave a wry smile. " What would you do? "

Ashe considered for a moment. " I think I'd probably hand it over to the police."

" That's exactly what I'm going to do," Winter said. The telephone rang. Winter grasped Ashe's hand. " There's my call at last. . . . Thank you for coming, old chap. . . . Will you excuse me? "

" I'll let myself out," Ashe said. " Good night. . . ."

Nancy was appalled when Ashe told her what Terry

had done—and quoted the contents of the note to her.

"As though Laurence hasn't had enough to put up with without that!" she said indignantly. "What a beastly letter!"

"Well, it could have been expressed less crudely, I agree," Ashe said. "As far as the substance goes, I'd had exactly the same idea—so I can hardly quarrel with that."

"At least you kept it to yourself—more or less. . . . I think it's horrible—and so absolutely typical. . . ."

"Terry's a rough chap and he writes roughly," Ashe said. "It was stupid to send a letter like that and he'll probably get into more trouble over it. . . . But if he thinks Laurence committed a murder that he's been virtually accused of himself, you'd hardly expect him to be polite."

"I'm sure he doesn't think anything of the sort," Nancy said. "He's simply trying to make things as unpleasant for Laurence as possible, and Sheila's gossip has given him the chance. . . . He's obviously eaten up with spite—by now he probably blames Laurence for everything that's happened to him. . . . Honestly, darling, I'm beginning to wonder if he's quite sane. . . ."

"The experts never doubted that he was."

"Then there's even less excuse for him. . . . Anyway, what did Laurence say about the letter?"

"He took it pretty calmly. . . ."

"Yes—well he would, of course. A man with nothing on his conscience wouldn't think it was important. Just very distasteful."

Ashe gave a half-hearted nod. He'd been impressed himself with Winter's behaviour. No protestations, no denials, no righteous indignation, no reminders of his fondness for his dead wife. . . . Just contempt. . . . Looking back, Ashe couldn't fault his attitude anywhere. . . . All the same, a guilty man might see his danger, and guard against it. A clever, guilty man. . . .

" I suppose he'll tell the police? " Nancy said.

" He says he's going to. . . ."

That was another thing that had given Ashe thought. Would a guilty man, he'd asked himself, want to take a letter like that to the police? Indeed, would he want to show it to anyone at all? Wouldn't he be more likely to destroy it and keep quiet? But, very soon, Ashe had seen that it wasn't as simple as that. . . .

" He'd probably have to take it to the police in any case," he said. " I mean, taking it doesn't prove his innocence. . . . The police might easily come to hear of it in other ways. Terry might send his accusation direct to them. He might spread it around. . . . Then the police would wonder why Laurence hadn't mentioned the letter in the first place. They'd think it was strange. A guilty man would probably feel he *had* to be frank about it. . . ."

Nancy looked at him in surprise. " Darling, what are you talking about? We *know* Laurence isn't guilty. . . ."

" Well . . ." Ashe hesitated.

" You said so yourself. You said he couldn't possibly have done it, because of the alibi."

" That's quite true, he couldn't. . . . But this evening I thought of another possibility. Laurence could have got someone else to do it for him. . . ." Without much conviction, he told Nancy the idea he'd had about Winter and John Cole.

She looked at him in disbelief. " Darling, this is the most fantastic thing yet. . . . You *can't* be serious."

" Oh, I know it's not likely," Ashe said. " It's the longest of long shots. . . ."

" Robert, it's preposterous! Think of the dangers, apart from anything else. . . . Choosing somebody practically at random, and proposing he should commit a murder for you! Whatever money you offered, you'd be taking a fearful risk by even mentioning it. . . . And if the man did agree to do it, you'd be putting your life in his hands. . . . It just doesn't make sense at all— it's too utterly absurd. . . ."

" I suppose it is," Ashe said.

" And, anyway, you've absolutely nothing to go on."

" Only my feeling about that alibi," Ashe agreed. He stood silent for a moment, frowning. " All the same, I think I'll just take a look at John Cole. . . ."

Ashe didn't know where Cole lived, but he soon found the address in the telephone directory. It was a place called Partridge Lane, about half-way between Ashe's house and Winter's. Ashe rang the number, spoke to a man who turned out to be Cole himself, and made an appointment to go and see him in the morning about some work he said he wanted doing.

At ten o'clock next day he drove over. He couldn't pretend even to himself that he expected much from the visit, but a little reconnaissance could do no possible harm. Once again, he'd promised Nancy to be very discreet.

Cole's place proved to be little more than a wooden shack on a brick foundation—something better than a shed, but definitely less than a bungalow. It stood on its own in a small rectangle of ground carved out of somebody's field. In the yard beyond the rutted entrance there was a small grey van, a tractor, various other pieces of farm machinery including what Ashe took by its appearance to be a blowing machine, a heap of sand, a pile of bricks, and a large stack of farm manure. Beside the gate there was a sign which said, "J. Cole, Farm Contractor." Ashe made a mental note that the sign looked fairly new.

John Cole emerged from the shed as he drove in. He was a tubby man of about thirty-five, with thinning hair. The sleeves of his plaid shirt were rolled up, revealing plump but muscular forearms.

" 'Morning," he said affably. " Mr. Ashe? "

Ashe nodded.

" Pleased to meet you. . . . You're the vet over at Springfield, aren't you? "

" That's right."

" I thought you must be. . . . Well, sir, what can I do for you? "

" It's quite a small job," Ashe told him. " I've a two-acre field behind my house and it's getting very sour. I wondered if you could spread some lime on it for me. . . . I believe you did the same thing for a friend of mine—Mr. Winter."

" That's so," Cole said. " Yes—I'd be glad to do it for you. . . ." His manner was brisk and businesslike, not slow like a countryman's. He hadn't a country accent, either—by his speech, he could have been from anywhere. It was the second point that Ashe noted.

For a few moments they discussed the job. Ashe described the field. Cole quoted a price. " You won't find anyone who'll do it cheaper than that," he said. " I'm well known round here for good value. . . ."

" It sounds reasonable enough," Ashe said. " That's fine, then. . . ." He gazed around in an amiable way. " You seem to have quite an active little business here. . . ."

" Oh, we do most things. Supply anything people want—sand, gravel, muck, cement. . . . Ploughing, harrowing, felling timber, clearing rough ground— we don't turn much down."

" You have someone to help you, have you? " Ashe casually offered Cole a cigarette, which he accepted.

" Yes, I employ one chap. . . . I'll be getting another pretty soon, if things go on as they are."

" Have you been at it long? "

" About a year. . . . I used to be in the building trade myself, but I had a bit of an accident and had to pack it in for a time—got blood poisoning. . . . Then when I was okay again I thought I'd like to start up something on my own."

" You prefer to be your own boss, eh? "

" Sure—who wouldn't? "

" Did you build this place yourself? "

" No, it was here already. . . . Bit of a dump, isn't it? But it was cheap, and it suits me all right. Just the ticket."

" You're not married? "

" Not me ! " Cole said. " I like my freedom."

So far Ashe had been only mildly interested—but at the word " freedom " something clicked. If Cole *had* had anything to do with the murder, Ashe thought, he would have needed freedom. Freedom from having other people around at night, freedom to come and go at will without being seen. . . . Was it by chance that, like Terry, he was living by himself in an isolated place? If Winter *had* wanted someone to do his dirty work for him, wasn't Cole perfectly situated to do it?

Cole was beginning to move towards the car. Ashe said, " Well, I mustn't keep you. . . ." He took a step or two—then stopped beside the blower. " Is this the machine you use? "

" That's right," Cole said. " The lime, or whatever it is, goes in here, and a band from the tractor works the blower . . . The stuff scatters around a lot in a wind—people often try to have the job done when they're away from home, if the field's near the house. . . . That's what Mr. Winter did."

Suspicion suddenly flared in Ashe. Maybe his journey hadn't been a waste of time after all. . . . Of course, avoidance of discomfort *could* have been the explanation of the Tuesday dusting at Winter's place, the so-convenient dusting in his absence. . . . But why that glib, gratuitous piece of information from Cole? As though the dusting on that particular day needed an excuse. . . .

" Shocking affair, that was," Cole was saying. " Nearly turned me up when I heard they'd found Mrs. Winter's body in the paddock. I reckon I must have been dusting within a few feet of it—might have run the tractor over it! It beats me how they came to let that fellow Booth go free."

" You think he did it? "

" I'm damn' sure he did it," Cole said, stubbing out his cigarette on the blower. " Sticks out a mile. . . ." He opened the car door and stood back. " Okay, Mr. Ashe—just give me a couple of days' notice when you're ready to have the liming done, and I'll be along. . . ."

Ashe didn't reply. He was staring in dismay at Cole's left hand.

Whoever had strangled Mavis Winter, it definitely wasn't Cole. The whole top joint of his left thumb was missing.

With his mind at last empty of theories, Ashe went on from the contractor's to make a number of calls on clients, which took up the rest of the morning. He returned home just before one, to find Inspector Mayo's car parked outside the house and the inspector sitting at the wheel with a newspaper, apparently waiting for him.

As he parked his own car and got out, Mayo walked slowly over to him. " Ah, here you are, Mr. Ashe. . . . Your wife said you wouldn't be long." The inspector was looking very grim.

" Anything wrong? " Ashe asked.

Mayo took from his pocket a letter which Ashe recognised as the one that Terry had sent to Winter. " I understand you know about this. . . ."

Ashe nodded. " Winter showed it to me. . . ."

" Booth's heading fast for more trouble," Mayo said. " You don't happen to know where he's to be found, I suppose? "

" If you mean his exact address, I'm afraid I don't, Inspector."

" H'm—I just wondered. . . . He's the 'no fixed abode' type, of course. But we'll trace him. . . . Anyway, that's not really what I came about."

" What did you come about, Inspector? "

" There's been altogether too much talk about this case, Mr. Ashe. Wild talk. . . . It seems that Booth got some of this scurrilous stuff from Sheila MacLean. I've just been giving her a dressing down. . . ." He tapped the letter. " There's no telling where this sort of thing might end. . . ."

Ashe said, " I deplore the letter, Inspector—but there's bound to be talk, surely, when so much is uncertain. . . ."

" There's nothing uncertain about Mr. Winter," Mayo said sharply. " He couldn't have killed his wife, as you know perfectly well. . . . I'm not sure how far you've encouraged this line of talk, but I suspect quite a bit. I'd remind you there's such a thing as criminal libel—you could be heading for bad trouble yourself. . . ."

He moved towards his car, turned at the door.

" You're a prison visitor and a responsible citizen, Mr. Ashe. You should know better than to give currency to vicious gossip. . . . Let's have no more of it."

The encounter left Ashe in a state of profound depression. He felt humiliated by Mayo's reprimand, and angry with himself for failing to answer it. If the conversation could have taken place again, he thought, there were things he could say. For instance, that Mayo hadn't hesitated himself to make pretty scurrilous allegations against Terry, who was technically as innocent as Winter. . . . But then Mayo, of course, had been doing his appointed duty, not just interfering. . . . And there really was a case against Terry. An increasingly strong case, to be honest. . . . Whereas there was none at all now against Laurence. There was merely an extraordinarily pat alibi that couldn't be got round—an alibi that still nagged at Ashe. . . . Nothing else. . . . The see-saw of evidence had come down heavily against Terry, and he could see no fresh lines of inquiry. There was really nothing more he could do. . . . And if he didn't drop the matter now, he probably would be in trouble. . . . Already, he thought gloomily, unfavourable reports about him were probably circulating in official quarters. A prison visitor of impaired judgment—over-zealous—too easily swayed by emotion. . . . No doubt he'd be getting that very polite letter of thanks for past services at the end of the year—without a renewed invitation to serve. . . . Oh, well, what the hell!

The afternoon brought no relief from his irritation and despondency. He knew he could expect no sympathy from Nancy, who had been upset by the inspector's visit and was now showing her own annoyance by a studied silence. Sheila, red-eyed after Mayo's sharp words, was made still more miserable when, by the afternoon post, she received another, re-addressed, letter from Terry, saying briefly that he'd had a row with the foreman of the building site and was going to look for something else. . . . To Ashe, the letter seemed the last straw. Hopeless fellow! Really, it was idiotic to waste any more thought on him. . . . Yet thought was hard to discipline.

He tried to do some work in the surgery, but he couldn't settle to it. He'd never felt less interested in animals. After tea he gave it up and drifted out of doors. Maybe he'd do some job in the garden—he usually found that soothing. Just the right weather for it, too—the September day was wonderful, sunny and very warm, as it had been for nearly a fortnight. The children, he saw, had spread a rug on a shady bit of the paved terrace and were playing some game with an impish boy named Michael who lived a couple of houses away and had been asked in for tea. Nancy was in a deck-chair, reading. Sheila, worn out by her troubles, had gone down to the lower lawn to have a nap.

Ashe got out the hose and started to sprinkle the parched grass below the terrace. It was a pleasant task in the heat—and the scent was delicious. . . . He'd only been at it for two minutes when the telephone rang. He put the hose down and went inside. . . . It was a Mrs. Chadwick—her budgie had caught its wing in its cage—it seemed to be broken. . . . Yes, Ashe said, she could bring it round in the morning. . . .

At that moment there was a yell from the garden. Bloody kids, Ashe thought. He went out, fuming. The scene was no longer peaceful. Michael had got hold of the hose and had sprayed the other children. Ashe grabbed the hose, and Nancy restored order. The girls were soon dried off. The wet rug was spread out in the sun. Jane's howls ceased. Margaret fetched a Li-lo and put it down where the rug had been and presently the children resumed their game.

Ashe went on with his watering.

It wasn't until later that he became conscious of a strange uneasiness in his mind—some new disturbance, quite different from his earlier irritation and depression. A much more positive thing. Something had happened, he felt, that was enormously important—but he

didn't know what it was, he couldn't place it. . . .
Something that afternoon. . . .

It came to him suddenly, as a sharp visual picture.
The children playing. . . . The dry oblong on the
wet paved terrace, where the rug had been taken
away. . . . And then the Li-lo, in the same spot, only a
slightly different shape. . . .

IV

Ashe curbed his impulse to rush at once across the garden and tell Nancy about the exciting new possibility that had suddenly opened up. In her present mood, he knew, she wouldn't take at all kindly to yet another unsupported flash of inspiration. He must think about it a little more on his own. He sat down in the shade and lit his pipe and forced himself to consider as calmly as he could just what might have happened. . . . To work out the implications. . . . He thought about it for quite a while. It was only when he felt he had at least some of the problems sorted out that he went over to Nancy and pulled up a deck-chair beside her.

" Darling, I've had an idea. . . ."

Nancy gave him a cold look. " If it's anything more about Laurence," she said, " I absolutely refuse to discuss it. You know what Inspector Mayo said. . . ."

" No, really, you must. . . . I believe I've thought of a way Laurence could have faked his alibi."

" Oh, Robert, of course he didn't."

" But he could have done."

" It's absurd. . . . How I wish you'd drop this stupid vendetta."

" It's not a vendetta," Ashe said. " I'm not trying to pin anything on him he didn't do. I simply want to get at the truth."

" You've got a bee in your bonnet about him—

really, it's becoming an obsession. You just can't let him alone."

"No, I can't," Ashe said, "not yet. I'm still not convinced he ought to be left alone. If he strangled his wife for her money, and faked an alibi for himself, and framed Terry so that he'd be blamed, then he's in-human—a monster—and if I can help it he's not going to get away with it. . . . Look, Nancy, pretend it isn't Laurence—pretend it's someone else I'm talking about. Anyone. Treat my idea as an exercise. Tear it to pieces if you like. Scoff at it—I don't care. But at least listen to it. . . . That's fair enough, surely?"

Reluctantly, Nancy put down her book. "Well— what is your idea?"

"It was the Li-lo over there that started it. . . . Looking at it now, you'd probably say that because it's about the same size and shape as the bit of terrace that was left dry when Michael shot that water over everything, and because it's roughly covering the same spot, it was there when the water was sprinkled. . . . But we know it wasn't—it was the rug that was sprinkled. . . . Do you see? The fact that there was no lime dust under Mavis's body doesn't necessarily mean the body was there when the liming was done. It only means that *something* was there. . . ."

Nancy gave a thoughtful nod.

"Well," Ashe said, getting into his stride, "suppose that before Laurence left home that week-end, he spread something out in the rough grass at the side of the paddock that was about the same size and shape as Mavis's body. Anything. An old raincoat, if you like. . . . Right. Then he goes off to Salfleet with Mavis. On the Monday afternoon he runs the boat aground in a place that makes an uncomfortable night certain, and he persuades Mavis to come home. From the moment she leaves he sticks to Ted Pettit like a leech so that every second of that Monday night is fully accounted for. On the Tuesday morning John Cole comes to the paddock in all innocence and does the liming according to instructions. Then Laurence comes back secretly, say on the Tuesday night, and kills Mavis, and substitutes the body for the raincoat. The police find there's no lime under it, so they naturally conclude it was lying there when the liming was done on the Tuesday morning—and Laurence has got his alibi."

" Wasn't there lime on top of the body? " Nancy said. " How would that have got there? "

" Oh, there wouldn't have been any problem about that. . . . The stuff would have been lying all around —Laurence could simply have scattered some over the body after the substitution."

" Would it have looked the same—as though it had been blown, I mean? "

" I don't see why not—he could have blown it from the palm of his hand so that it fell evenly. . . . Anyway, no one would have given that a thought when the body was first found—and once it had been moved it would have been too late."

" Suppose the police hadn't noticed that there was no lime under the body—then where would the alibi have been? "

" Well, Laurence was there," Ashe said, " he could easily have drawn someone's attention to it if necessary. . . . But it's not the sort of thing the police would miss."

" M'm. . . . Anyhow, I shouldn't think it would be very easy to arrange a thing like a raincoat into the exact size and shape of a body."

" There wouldn't have been any need to make it exact," Ashe said. " No one could possibly know for certain just how the lime dust would have blown and settled—the edges of the bare space would have been pretty irregular anyway. It wouldn't be like a snowfall. . . . The general outline would have been enough. No one would have thought to question it. . . ."

" Well—it's ingenious," Nancy admitted. " *Very* ingenious. . . . But I'm sure it didn't happen."

" Don't be too sure," Ashe said. " I've not finished yet. . . . It would explain all those things that seemed so odd when we were thinking of Terry as the murderer. Remember we were surprised at the fact that he'd apparently made off up the paddock when it didn't lead anywhere and he could have got away at the front. . . . At least, *I* was. . . . But if the liming was an essential part of a faked alibi, the body would have *had* to be up in the paddock, and everything else would have had to be arranged accordingly. . . . Then there was the business of the body being carried into the long grass—which always seemed so pointless to me if Terry was the murderer. . . . But if Laurence was, and if the idea was that the body was supposed to be lying there when the liming was done, then the chosen place *had* to be in the grass and not on the path, because otherwise the contractor would have been able to say that it definitely *hadn't* been there when he did the liming. . . . You see how well things begin to tie in."

"You're forgetting something that doesn't tie in," Nancy said. "The medical evidence. . . . According to that, Mavis *was* killed on the Monday night, or thereabouts."

Ashe grunted. "I know that's a bit awkward—but as I said before, it's fairly easy to make a mistake about the time of death. . . ."

"Not a mistake of twenty-four hours, surely—not over such a short period? Anyway, I'm sure Monday *was* the night. If Mavis had still been alive on the Tuesday morning, something would have been seen or heard of her. She wouldn't have stayed shut up in the house all day, not showing herself to anyone, not even to Cole when he came to do the dusting. . . . She'd almost certainly have gone shopping—or at least telephoned a tradesman or two. . . . And I should think she'd have fetched her dog back from the kennels—especially if there was a chance of a second night there alone. . . ."

Ashe nodded, frowning. "Yes, that's all true. . . . And if Mavis had done any of those things, Laurence's alibi would have gone for a burton. . . . He'd have seen the danger beforehand, too—he'd never have taken such a chance. . . ."

"Then that's really the end of it, isn't it?" Nancy said.

Ashe was silent. It did almost seem to be the end. . . . Doggedly, he sought for a way through the block—and logic, for an over-sanguine moment, seemed to suggest one. . . .

"Let's agree that Mavis *was* dead by the Monday night," he said. "Laurence killed her—that's the premise. But Laurence was at Salfleet all the time till

then. . . . That means he must have killed her at Salfleet and brought the body up later!''

"But, Robert, we know she left by car on the
Monday evening. . . ."

"We know Ted Pettit heard Laurence say something about driving carefully," Ashe said. "That's a
bit different. He could have been talking loudly to
thin air. . . ."

"Well, we know the car left. Ted heard it being
driven off—and it wasn't there next day. And next
time it was seen it was at home in the garage. And
Laurence had to come back by train. That's all pretty
good evidence."

"Oh . . . yes, of course. . . . *Blast!*"

"Anyway," Nancy said, "to get back for a minute
to your liming alibi. . . . I just can't believe that any
murderer would have dared to depend on it. . . . If the
liming could have been done, and checked up on,
before the murder, that might have been different.
But surely no murderer would have relied on it with
a body already on his hands. Suppose Cole had
decided that it wasn't convenient for him to do it on
the Tuesday after all. . . ."

Ashe nodded dolefully. It was the point that had
occurred to him earlier—but to-day, in his new
enthusiasm, he'd lost sight of it.

"Or suppose it had rained?"

"The weather was settled," Ashe said. "For that
matter, rain might have provided as good an alibi
as the lime—there'd have been a dry patch of
ground under the raincoat, or whatever it was,
and the body could easily have been wetted on top.
Still . . ."

" Suppose Cole hadn't dusted near enough to where the raincoat had been put? Suppose he'd started his dusting on that side of the paddock, and blown the lime in the *other* direction? Suppose he'd happened to stroll into the long grass—then he'd have known the body wasn't there, and afterwards he'd have said so. . . . I can't imagine any murderer accepting these risks. . . . As I see it, the dusting would only have made a safe alibi if the man who did it had been an accomplice— and therefore absolutely reliable. . . ."

Ashe stared at her. Again, she'd worked round to an earlier idea of his—but with a difference. He'd mentally written Cole out of the case after he'd found that the man was physically incapable of having strangled Mavis. Now he suddenly wondered if he'd been premature.

" That's quite a thought," he said. " A man wouldn't need two thumbs to be an accomplice."

" But there's nothing whatever to suggest that Cole *was* an accomplice." Nancy looked as though she wished she hadn't mentioned it. She'd never even begun to take Ashe's Cole idea seriously.

" I don't know," Ashe said, " he struck me as a pretty smooth customer. I didn't really take to him at all. . . ."

" Darling, you can't honestly think it's possible . . . ! How could it happen? How could the subject ever have been brought up in the first place? Can you really imagine Laurence or anyone else going along to Cole and saying, 'I'd like you to join me in a plot to kill my wife and I'll pay you well?' Just as though it was another contract job! It's too silly. . . . There'd have to be a very close association before anyone would dream of making a suggestion like that. . . . No one would dare to suggest it to a stranger."

" We don't know that Laurence and Cole *were* strangers," Ashe said. " The fact is, we know nothing about Cole—except that he's not a countryman, and he lives very conveniently alone, and his business is fairly new. . . . All rather suspicious circumstances."

" His business may be new, but you said yourself it seemed genuine. . . . Rather flourishing, you thought. And it's not so unusual for men of that sort to live alone in the country. . . . Or for people who aren't born countrymen to set up businesses in the country— often they're the ones with most initiative. . . . Really, darling, you must admit the case against Cole couldn't be thinner. It's practically non-existent."

" If we knew more it might not be," Ashe persisted. " I still say the possibility can't be ruled out. . . . And, of course, if Cole *was* Laurence's accomplice, that would alter everything. We'd be back again with the possibility that Mavis was killed at Salfleet. . . . It could have been *Cole* who drove the car away in the dark on the Monday evening."

" You're just piling one speculation on another," Nancy said.

" I know I am—but that's the only way to make any progress when there are hardly any facts. And there is a certain sense in it all. . . . Let's go back a bit now and see where we've got to. . . . We know that Mavis was alive on the Monday afternoon, because she went ashore with Laurence and Ted Pettit saw her. And soon after dusk Laurence was ashore again to report the grounding, and after that he didn't leave Ted. . . . So if he killed Mavis at Salfleet, it must have been during the interval—early on the Monday evening. That would square reasonably well with the medical evidence. . . ."

" You accept the medical evidence when it suits you! "

" Why not? It's nice to be in step for a change. . . . He could have killed her on the boat—you couldn't have a safer, more private place than that. Anchored in some quiet spot. . . . And, Nancy, that would explain another thing—the fact that Mavis was strangled. It never sounded to me like Terry—but it would be the way for Laurence. He certainly wouldn't have wanted any traces of blood on the boat. . . . You must agree that all these small points do add up."

" I agree you're making the best of your material," Nancy said. " Anyway—go on. . . . What would he have done with the body afterwards? "

" He could have hidden it in the saltings. They'd be the perfect place—there are lots of deep rills. . . ."

" When would he have gone back for it? "

" The next night, I suppose—after dark."

Nancy shook her head. " I can't see him leaving it in the saltings for a whole day. The place may be lonely, but there were other boats around, or there could have been. Someone might have landed, and found it. . . . In any case, I shouldn't think he'd have had time to hide it in the saltings—not safely. . . . He was ashore talking to Ted soon after dark—and landing a body, even a small one, from a boat single-handed wouldn't be a very quick operation, would it? It seems to me that he'd have had to start it in daylight—

and in daylight he might have been seen. It all sounds far too dangerous."

" M'm. . . . Maybe you're right. . . . Well, he could have kept the body *on* the boat, I suppose."

" What, all night—when he knew Ted Pettit would be going out there? "

" The boat must have at least two cabins," Ashe said, " or there wouldn't have been room for Sheila when she went down. . . . Laurence could have put the body in one of them and covered it with a rug or something and locked the door. . . . After all, Ted was a sort of employee—he wouldn't have gone wandering about the boat on his own. And he said he and Laurence slept in the saloon. . . ."

" It would have been very daring."

" If Laurence did any of the things we're supposing he may have done," Ashe said, " he must have all the nerve in the world. . . . So let's say he did keep the body on the boat overnight."

" He'd still have had to get it to the paddock," Nancy said. " And he hadn't a car."

" I know—that's the next problem. . . ." Ashe considered for a while. " Yes, I can see a way," he said finally.

" Well? "

" If Cole was his accomplice, there'd have been no difficulty at all. Cole could have gone down in that van of his on the Tuesday evening—to some pre-arranged rendezvous, some lonely place. . . . According to the map, there are several places where minor tracks lead down to the water. . . . He could have helped Laurence get the body ashore from the boat, and driven him to the house with it. Laurence could have substituted the body for whatever was already in the paddock, fixed the house to give the impression of a breaking-in by Terry according to the plan he'd already made, set the scene generally, and been driven back again to the boat by Cole. . . . Then Cole would have come home, and Laurence would have taken the boat to its mooring on the Wednesday morning and caught the train home."

" It sounds a hard night for Cole," Nancy said. " Could he have done all those journeys in the time? "

" Well, let's see. . . . Say three hours for the trip. If he'd first left here at dusk, he'd have been at the rendezvous about eleven. Half an hour to get the body from the boat to the van—eleven-thirty. Three hours back—two-thirty. Half an hour to make the substitution and set the scene at the house—three o'clock. Three hours to Salfleet with Laurence—six o'clock. . . . Three hours back alone—nine o'clock. . . . That sounds all right. As far as the logistics are concerned, I don't see any problem at all."

" *If* Cole was an accomplice. . . ."

" Exactly."

" And *if* Mavis didn't drive home alone on the Monday night. . . . You'll probably find now that Ted Pettit heard Mavis's voice at the car. And that'll be the end of your house of cards."

" Will you take a bet? " Ashe said. " I can soon ask him. . . ." He got up and strode off towards the house.

" For heaven's sake be careful what you say," Nancy called after him.

She waited, looking down at her book but not

reading it. Ashe was away about five minutes. He returned serious-faced.

"You've lost your bet, haven't you?" Nancy said.

"No—*you* have. . . . All Ted heard was Laurence saying, 'You'll drive carefully, darling, won't you. . . .' He didn't hear Mavis's voice. And he didn't see anything except the car lights—it was too dark. . . . Incidentally, he *didn't* go all over Laurence's boat that night—there's an after cabin he didn't go into. . . . That means, Nancy, we've produced a theory of what might have happened without a single obvious flaw in it."

Nancy sat silent for a while. Then she said, "The flaw, of course, is that it's just a piece of fiction. . . . It's intriguing fiction, I agree—but from beginning to end it's something you've made up to suit a preconceived idea."

"It fits the facts in a lot of places."

"Because you've forced it to. . . . Darling, you know as well as I do that there isn't a jot of real evidence. You've absolutely nothing against Cole—nothing whatever. You've turned him into a murderer's accomplice because he happened to lime a field, which is his job! As for Laurence—well, you've just had an imaginative spree, that's all. You've nothing solid against him. It would be different if you'd caught him out in anything—some lie, some discrepancy—but you haven't. It's a completely unreal case. . . ."

"I'd say it's as good as the case against Terry," Ashe said. "There was nothing solid to go on there, either—it was all supposition."

"Perhaps so—but if the choice is between a sordid

attack by someone like Terry, and a calculated plot by Laurence, the first seems far more likely."

" To you, but not to me. . . . Well, there it is—you reject my theory, and I stick to it. . . . The thing now is—how can I *test* it?"

" I don't see how you possibly can."

" There's Cole, of course—I could try and dig into his background a bit. . . . Find out where he came from, what he was doing before, what his record is. . . ." Ashe frowned. " That's really a job for the police, though."

" I certainly can't see Inspector Mayo helping with it," Nancy said.

" No, you're right. . . . Of course, a private inquiry agent could do it."

" Well, we're not going to spend money on an inquiry agent," Nancy said indignantly. " That's right out! Just for a wild-goose chase. . . . Besides, it would be sure to lead to trouble. . . . Look, Robert, you said this was going to be an exercise. . . . If you start probing into people's private lives, people who live round here and whom you've got absolutely nothing against, it won't be long before we have to leave. . . . You could ruin us! And for what? Just a stubborn notion. . . ."

" Well, maybe there's some other way," Ashe said. " Some simpler way. . . . All we need is one bit of material evidence. . . . Damn it, all that activity couldn't have happened without leaving a trace. . . ."

" It could if it was imaginary."

" That's just it—a trace would prove it wasn't. . . . They say murderers usually make a mistake, Nancy—

and in a complicated plot like this I should think it would have been very easy to make one. . . . All those comings and goings, the secret meetings there must have been, the moving of the body, the substitution, the scattering of the lime. . . . Lime! Now that's a thought. . . . I wonder what happened to whatever was used as a substitute for the body."

" If it ever existed," Nancy said, " it was probably destroyed. Cole could have taken it away. . . ."

" It would have had lime on it. There might be traces in his van. . . ."

" There would be anyway, darling, if he was using the stuff a lot. . . ."

" Yes—of course. . . . Wait a minute, though—what about Laurence? If he was out there in the dark in a limed paddock, and was actually scattering lime over a body, he must have got some of it on him—on his clothes. . . . And if he wasn't supposed to be there . . ."

" He was supposed to be there after the body was found," Nancy said, " moving about the paddock, showing the police around—all quite legitimately. . . . I should think there might well be traces of lime on some of his clothes—but they certainly wouldn't prove anything. . . ."

" True. . . ." Ashe relapsed into silence again. Then he suddenly gave a sharp exclamation. " I know what would, though! "

" What? "

" A trace of lime on the boat. . . . Laurence hasn't been back there since he left it on the Wednesday—officially he hasn't been on it since he first came in contact with the lime. . . . So one speck of the stuff found there would prove he'd been secretly in the paddock when he was supposed to be at Salfleet. It would be clear evidence of his guilt."

" Would you expect to find any—if he was guilty? Wouldn't he have cleaned himself up before he went back? "

" Maybe—maybe not. . . . Once he'd made the substitution and set the scene at the house, I doubt if he'd have wanted to hang about there a moment longer than was necessary. I certainly can't see him switching on lights and taking a bath when the house was supposed to be unoccupied. . . . He'd have been more likely to go straight back to the boat and clean up there. Especially as, by our calculations, there wouldn't have been any time to spare."

" He might not have gone near the lime himself, of course," Nancy said. " Cole might have done all that part. . . ."

Ashe shook his head. " I can't imagine Laurence not wanting to make sure that the body was placed just in the right spot, with the right amount of lime scattered over it. . . . His neck was at stake—he'd have checked, at the very least. . . ."

" Well," Nancy said, " it's an idea—but I don't see what you can do about it."

" The obvious thing is to go down to Salfleet and row out to the boat and put a vacuum cleaner over it. . . ."

" You mean break in! Robert, you must be off your head. If you're not careful you'll finish up in prison yourself, with someone visiting you! "

" Well, somebody ought to. . . ."

" It's not going to be you. . . . Robert, this is

where I absolutely put my foot down. You simply can't. . . ."

Ashe frowned. " I wonder if I could get Mayo to do it. . . . It wouldn't be like asking him to make a lot of vague inquiries that would take time and money. It would be one specific thing—an hour's work. . . . And with a definite result, one way or the other."

" I shouldn't think he would for a moment," Nancy said. " And I wouldn't like to be there when you asked him! He couldn't have made his attitude clearer. . . ."

The ringing of the telephone interrupted them. Nancy went to answer it. When she emerged a moment or two later she didn't look very pleased.

" It's Terry," she said. " He wants to talk to Sheila."

" To Sheila? How did he know she was here? "

" He says he rang Mrs. Dyson's, and one of the children told him. . . ."

" I see. . . ." Ashe half rose. " Maybe I'll have a word with him, too. . . ."

Alarm showed on Nancy's face. " Darling, what's the point? . . . Where is Sheila, do you know? "

" She was asleep on a Li-lo last time I saw her."

Nancy called " Sheila! " There was an answering call from the lower lawn, and Sheila appeared, rubbing her eyes, a little flushed.

" Terry's on the phone," Nancy said.

" Give him my regards! " Ashe told her. He subsided into his chair. " You know," he said to Nancy, " I think I *will* put it to Mayo in the morning. I'll try to talk him round. . . . It's our one chance."

Nancy's mouth tightened. " I think you're asking

for trouble. And I'm sure you're quite wrong about Laurence."

" *I'm* sure that Terry didn't kill Mavis," Ashe said. " I've never been surer. . . ."

Sleep came belatedly to Ashe that night. The long, constructive argument with Nancy, the mental acrobatics it had required, had left him stimulated rather than tired. Now he found it impossible to switch his mind from the subject. For hours he lay awake, going again over every detail of the case against Winter, probing for any weaknesses he might have overlooked. But the more he thought about it, the more convinced he felt that he'd arrived at something very near the truth. The pattern of his theory was so neat, the logic so satisfying. If there had been only one or two pointers to Winter's guilt, he might have had doubts— but surely so many in conjunction were conclusive. Coincidence could hardly explain them. . . . In his mind he went over the salient ones again, weighing them, savouring them. . . . Winter's immensely powerful motive—money. The way he'd practically asked for a tough ex-prisoner—as though anyone, without an ulterior motive, would have gone that far in charity! The way he'd fixed up Terry in the cottage. The way he'd invited him repeatedly to his house—to give him, of course, the necessary knowledge of the establishment. His near-accusation of office-breaking, without a shadow of proof. The pressure on Sheila to go home for the week-end. The peculiarities of the actual murder events, which only guilt on Winter's part could satisfactorily explain. The extreme unlikelihood that Mavis would have returned

to that empty house alone. The too-perfect alibi. . . .
And much, much more. All of it fitting like a glove.
All of it interlocking. A massive, circumstantial in-
dictment. . . .

As Ashe's conviction grew, so did his anger at the
part that Winter had played. It wasn't only *what* he'd
done—it was the way in which he'd done it. The false
front of good-natured friendship, the pretence of really
caring about Terry's welfare, the sustained duplicity.
. . . What an act he'd put on! It made Ashe writhe
now to think with what subtle skill he'd seemed to
hesitate over taking Terry, blowing hot and cold,
letting himself appear to be persuaded when it was
already a resolved event; to think of the earnest discussion they'd had about Terry after the office-breaking; to think how deeply Winter had seemed to be
moved by Mavis's death, how perfectly he'd simulated
the dazed bereavement of a loving husband. The
hypocrite—the crafty, plotting hypocrite! But so
brilliantly clever! Why, he'd almost made Ashe believe
in Terry's guilt. . . .

With relief, Ashe turned his mind to Terry. The
reverse side of the picture. Terry had had no adequate
motive for anything. That was plain enough now.
Breaking into the house for a few pounds—who would
have done that when retribution was certain? And
the slashing—who would have cut his mark on everything so stupidly? And committing the murder—
when it could so easily have been avoided. All those
bits of inexplicable behaviour. . . . *Of course* it had been
a frame-up. Ashe marvelled that it had taken him so
long to realise it. Hadn't it stuck out a mile, from the
very beginning?

He wished now that he'd been stronger in his attitude, more positive, more thrusting. He oughtn't to
have been swayed so much by Nancy. He'd wavered
unforgivably. He should have followed his instinct,
he should have had more faith in Terry. He should
have realised that there was no more violence in the
boy. Terry *had* reformed—and he'd shown it. Until
the trouble had started, he'd been getting along splen-
didly. His behaviour had been very good until Winter
had started his tricks. . . . Well, fairly good. . . . He
had got Sheila in the family way—but at least he'd
always meant to marry her. . . . And no one could say
that he wasn't behaving decently now—writing to her,
ringing her up, keeping in touch. Sheila had been
much more cheerful again after that talk with him to-
night. Of course, he'd made mistakes—the tone of that
letter to Winter *had* been unpleasant. But there'd been
enough provocation. . . . And if he'd quarrelled with
his foreman in his new job, it was probably only because of the strain he was under. . . . Many people
would have cracked altogether. Once this case was
cleared up—as it was going to be—Terry would be a
new man. . . . Basically, he was good material. . . .
Mayo couldn't have been more wrong about
him. . . .

Mayo. . . . That was the next problem. How best
to approach him? A telephone call after breakfast,
perhaps—around nine, when he'd just have reached
his office. A confident mention of new evidence—a
request for an immediate interview. Mayo would
hardly be able to refuse it. Reprimand or no, Ashe still
had some status. . . . Then a summary of the case
against Winter—brought up to date, and introducing

John Cole. A brisk summary—because Mayo would be short of patience to start with. A forceful, pungent re-statement. . . . And then a request—no, a *demand*—that the boat should be checked for lime. . . . A suggestion that if it wasn't done there'd be a neglect of duty. . . . Who was Mayo, anyway? Ashe could be outspoken, too, when it was necessary . . . And it *was* necessary. . . . He'd get that boat examined, even if it meant a flaming row. . . . Even if it meant going to the Director of Public Prosecutions, the Home Secretary!

Ashe grimaced to himself. He was being a big fellow, wasn't he? Still, he'd do it. He hadn't any choice.

Slowly, he began to relax. He'd taken his decision now. He'd got everything sorted out. He lay quietly, listening to the wind. It seemed to be getting up. Rain was beginning to spatter on the windows, too. He ought to have looked at his barometer before he'd watered those lawns! His last thought, as he dozed off, was that if it had rained a few hours earlier he would never have realised that Winter's alibi had been faked. . . .

He woke next morning with his determination un-weakened. The slight elation of the night had passed, but his theory still looked as good to him in the cold, damp light of day as it had in the early hours. He felt eager and expectant, and could hardly wait to tackle Mayo. Through breakfast he was tensely preoccupied, mentally marshalling his phrases. By nine he was ready for the first approach. He would get the call over, he thought, before starting his surgery. . . . Then the arrival of a neighbour in distress delayed him. It was a Mrs. Percy, with a tabby that had been badly mauled in a night fight. . . . Ashe dressed its wounds and made it comfortable, hiding his impatience. The telephone rang, and he groaned inwardly. Was this going to be one of those days?

Nancy came in. "It's Inspector Mayo," she said.

Ashe gave her a startled look. "All right, I'll come. . . ." He put the tabby back in its basket. "He'll get over it, Mrs. Percy—just keep him warm and let him rest. . . . Good-bye."

He went quickly to the phone. "Hullo, Inspector."

"Hullo, Mr. Ashe." Mayo sounded strangely affable. "It's early to disturb you, but I've had some news from the Yard that I think you should know. . . ."

"Oh?"

"That protégé of yours—Booth. He hasn't changed his spots. . . . It's a great pity we couldn't have got him for the Winter murder—and spared another victim. . . ."

"Oh, no!" Ashe slumped down on the chair beside the phone. "What's happened?"

"He attacked a man outside a pub last night—slugged him with half a brick. Then he made off in a stolen car and wrecked it. I haven't all the details yet but the victim sounds in a fairly bad way. . . . I thought you'd better know the worst. . . . Something of the sort was bound to happen, of course, especially after he'd killed Mrs. Winter and got away with it.

. . . Anyhow, this time we should be able to put him away for years. . . ."

Ashe dropped the receiver and sat on by the phone, a hunched and beaten man. An abject man. . . . To have been wrong after all!—and just when he'd been so sure he was right. In this moment of disillusionment and defeat, his mind was filled with a bitterness he'd never known before. All the time and effort he'd spent on Terry in the prison—wasted. All the work and energy put into befriending him, encouraging him, watching over him after his release—gone for nothing. All the faith and belief in him after the murder—contemptuously betrayed. The deceit of the fellow, the ingratitude. . . . Ashe felt bruised, utterly humiliated. . . .

He was still sitting there, head in hands, when Nancy—wondering at the silence—came to see what was going on. " Darling, what is it?—what's the matter? "

He spat out the news like poison. " Terry's bashed someone else. . . ." In harsh, staccato words, he told her what Mayo had said.

" Oh, *Robert*! " Her hand went out to him, touched his shoulder in a gesture of tenderness. " Darling, I'm *so* sorry. . . ."

" The bloody little swine! " Ashe exploded. " I trusted him—and now he has to do this. . . . God, what a fool I've been! What a fool! "

" You mustn't say that," Nancy said. " *I* don't think so. . . . In a way you've been—wonderful. . . . And you might have been right."

Ashe shook his head. " I kidded myself—all the

time. I can see that now. I wanted to believe, so I did. . . . You said I was credulous, and you were damn' right. . . . I'm just a lousy judge of people."

" Not always. . . . Often you're not. It was simply that Terry meant so much to you. . . . Darling, you really don't have to blame yourself."

" Of course I do! God—when I think of the things I've said. All that stuff about Laurence. How *could* I have done? I must have been out of my mind."

" At least you only said it to me."

" It was a hell of a near thing." Ashe dabbed at his damp forehead. " If that phone hadn't rung, I'd have been pouring it all out to Mayo any minute. . . . God, what a thought! "

" Well, it did ring," Nancy said, " so there's nothing to worry about."

" I'm not so sure. . . ." Ashe looked at her in dismay. " I've spread an awful lot of dirt around about Laurence—I've talked to Sheila about him, and Mayo. . . . And I think he suspects I have. I suppose I'll have to go and grovel to him."

" You'll do nothing of the sort," Nancy said. " The best thing now is to forget the whole thing."

" That's not going to be easy."

" But you must, darling. It's finished—it's all over. . . . And it's silly to take it to heart. Laurence hasn't really come to any harm through what you've said. And if Terry's turned out a failure, the next man probably won't. Just stop thinking about it and concentrate on something else. Start being a busy vet again! "

Ashe gave a wry nod. " Yes, I've certainly neglected

the job. . . . What a waste it's all been! Those stupid arguments. . . . I must have been a hell of a trial to you, Nancy."

She smiled. " Not really, darling—not more than usual."

Ashe forced a grin. " Okay—*I* know. . . ." He took a long, deep breath. " All right, then—it's over. . . . Except that somebody's got to break the news to Sheila—poor kid! "

Nancy gave him an odd look. " I'll tell her," she said. She went out into the garden. Ashe walked slowly back to his surgery.

He had barely left the hall when the telephone rang again. He turned and walked back to it and picked up the receiver. " Robert Ashe here," he said.

" It's Mayo." The inspector's voice was no longer affable—it was sharp with urgency. " Something very odd seems to have been happening, Mr. Ashe. . . . I've had some more details—about young Booth. . . ."

" Well? "

" The attack I was telling you about seems to have occurred near that pub at Salfleet."

" At Salfleet! "

" That's right. . . . And the man who was attacked was that contractor fellow, John Cole. . . . It was his van that Booth crashed."

" *Cole!* " Ashe almost shouted the word. " Cole at Salfleet! "

" It's very strange. . . ."

" Inspector, I must see you. . . ." Ashe was almost beside himself with excitement.

" I'd very much like to see you," Mayo said. " The

thing is, I'm leaving right away for Salfleet—Booth and Cole are both in the South Essex hospital near-by. . . . Booth was knocked out in the crash but they think he'll be able to talk very soon. . . . Could you possibly meet me at the hospital, do you think? "

" *Could* I ! " Ashe exclaimed. " I'm practically there."

'V

COLE AT SALFLEET! All the way down to Essex, it was that phrase that hammered in Ashe's head. He couldn't begin to imagine what had taken the contractor there, what strange new turn had brought Cole and Terry together there and ended in this violent clash—but it had happened, and that was enough. Cole at Salfleet!—and he shouldn't have been. Incredibly, the see-saw had tilted Terry's way again. Ashe could scarcely wait to fire his questions. . . .

He did the journey to the hospital in a hundred and sixty minutes, flogging his old car mercilessly. Mayo was in conference with an Essex C.I.D. officer and a uniformed sergeant when he arrived. A message had been left with the porter, and he was shown in at once. The inspector shook hands rather self-consciously. " Good of you to come, Mr. Ashe." He introduced the others.

" How's Terry? " Ashe asked.

" He's doing well. He's come round. . . ."

" Have you talked to him? "

" Not yet. The doctor wanted to give him another check-up before we got to work on him. Any minute now. . . ."

" What about Cole? "

" He's not as badly hurt as they thought at first— but he won't be able to talk for a couple of days, at least."

" Then you don't know yet what happened? "

" Not everything, no—but we know more than we did last night. Inspector Ellis here had to piece things together as best he could—that's why the first account I gave you on the phone wasn't complete. . . . I'll tell you the story now as far as it goes. . . . About one o'clock this morning the people in the pub at Salfleet heard a crash out in the road. They went to investigate and found a van badly smashed and an unconscious man at the wheel. They rang for the police and an ambulance. Booth was identified by the insurance card he was carrying. He didn't have a driving licence on him. The log book in the crashed van was in the name of John Cole. The name didn't mean anything to the local chaps. . . . Then, soon after daylight, another unconscious man was found at the side of the road a hundred yards from the pub. His head had been battered and there was a blood-stained half-brick beside him. According to his driving licence, *he* was John Cole. So it began to look like an assault by Booth and an attempted getaway in Cole's van. . . . The local police checked with the Yard to see if Booth had a record—and the Yard got in touch with me. . . . Unfortunately they didn't mention John Cole by name until later. . . . By the way, this was found in Booth's pocket. . . ."

From a case beside him, Mayo produced a coloured handkerchief, knotted to form a small container at the end. He untied it, and spread it out carefully on the table. It held what looked like a handful of floor sweepings.

For a moment, Ashe stared at it as though he couldn't believe his eyes. So *that* was what Terry had been

doing. But how on earth . . . ? Then, slowly, light
dawned.

" Of course," he said. He looked at Mayo. " Inspector, I can tell you everything now. . . . Well,
almost everything. . . ."

" I'm glad to hear it," Mayo said. " Carry on, Mr.
Ashe."

Terry was sitting propped up in bed behind screens
when Ashe and the policeman went in to talk to
him half an hour later. He had a bandage round
his head, covering one eye, and another on his left
hand. His uncovered eye looked warily at Mayo,
but when it switched to Ashe it was friendly. Ashe
said, " Hullo, Terry," and Terry said " Hullo " and
grinned.

The sergeant took out a note-book. Mayo said,
" We'd like you to tell us what happened last night,
Booth. Everything—from the beginning."

" You goin' to charge me with anything? "

" I shouldn't think so. . . ."

" Okay," Terry said. He turned his head a little,
towards Ashe. " It was Sheila put me on to it, Mr.
Ashe. She heard what you was saying—you and Mrs.
Ashe. In the garden. All about Winter and Cole,
and how they could 'ave done it together, like, and
that maybe there was lime on the boat. She told me
on the phone, while you was still sitting out there. The
lot. . . ."

Ashe nodded. He'd already concluded that Sheila
must have been listening in the garden, not sleep-
ing.

" She said as how you thought the cops wouldn't

do anything about it," Terry went on, " and I didn't reckon they would either. So I thought I'd 'ave a bash at it myself, see. I got the bike out and biked over to Salfleet and got there in the middle of the night. It was lousy weather, raining and blowing, but it was pretty light, I reckon there was a moon somewhere, and after a bit I found a rowing-boat with some oars in it and got in and rowed out to where Sheila had said Winter's boat was. I had a hell of a job finding it, I can tell you—the bloody creek was stiff with them. . . . Any rate, I did find it in the end and I broke in—well, I had to, see—and I shook out all the rugs and cushions and bedding and stuff on to the floor and swept up the dust—same as you wanted to, Mr. Ashe. . . . Then I rowed back. . . ."

Sweat showed on his forehead. The nurse wiped it away and gave him a drink. Mayo said in a kindly voice, " Take your time, son."

Terry's visible eye blinked disbelievingly. " Blimey! " he said. " Well, any rate, I just got to the edge of the water when a van drove up with its lights doused. I thought that was pretty funny, specially at one o'clock in the morning, so I kep' still and watched. After a bit two men got out, and one of them was Winter."

" *Winter!* " Ashe shot a quick glance at Mayo.

" That's right. . . . He was talkin' sort of quiet but I'd know that bastard's voice if he only whispered. . . . Well, I was going to lie low and see what they were up to but they came walking over to where I was an' Winter suddenly saw there was someone in the boat and he came close and looked at me and said, ' What the devil are you doing here? ' I knew I was for it, then, with the two of them—I reckoned they'd try to do me in. I thought of letting out a yell but the nearest place was the pub an' that wasn't very near and I guessed they wouldn't hear me. So I tipped myself out of the boat and tried to beat it along the shore but they caught up with me—an' then there was a hell of a scrap. . . ." A cyclopean gleam came into Terry's eye. " I knocked Winter down and Cole knocked me down—I didn't know it was Cole then, I jus' reckoned it was—and he started kicking me and I grabbed something off the ground and jumped up and socked him with it—and, boy, he went out like a light. . . . Then I did beat it. I beat it for the van while Winter was still staggering around and I drove off in it. All I could think of was getting away, see. . . . After that I don't properly remember . . . I jus' remember feeling queer. I guess I'd been hurt more than I knew in the fight. . . ."

" You drove off the road," Mayo said. " Into a wall. . . . You must have passed out at the wheel."

Terry nodded. " What happened to Winter? "

" He seems to have cleared off."

" The bastard! Did you find the dust? "

" Yes."

" I hope it hangs him. . . . How's Cole? "

" Worse than you, but he'll get over it."

" I wouldn't care if he didn't," Terry said. He lay back on his pillow. " Cor, I feel bloody tired."

They left at the nurse's nod, well satisfied. They had got all they needed, Ashe thought—certainly more than he'd expected. The discovery that Winter had been at Salfleet, too, really clinched the matter. Ashe

felt a deep relief, rather than jubilation. Terry's story
had been pretty grim, the whole case had been horrible. The hope and shock and renewed hope of the
past few hours had been a tremendous strain. Now that
things had been so nearly sorted out, Ashe was beginning to suffer a reaction. . . .

" Well, that's it, Inspector, isn't it? " he said, as
they walked together to the cars. " You can't surely
doubt any more that it was Winter who killed his
wife? '

" M'm—we'll have to check on the dust, of course,"
Mayo said. " But what with your theory and Booth's
facts, it does look very likely indeed."

Ashe smiled. " You're a cautious bird, aren't you? "
He was silent for a moment. " I wonder why Winter
and Cole went to Salfleet. . . ."

" I'll be very interested to hear Winter's explanation."

" You'll be lucky to get the chance," Ashe said.
" After what happened last night, he must know he's
finished. He's probably on his way to South America
by now."

" I doubt it."

" What makes you say that? "

" Well, Mr. Ashe, I may have been slow to accept
your view about Winter, but I'm not slow about
everything. . . . As you said yourself, ' Cole at Salfleet . . . ! ' It sounded a most curious link, and it set
me thinking. I decided I couldn't ignore it. When I
rang you the second time I'd already sent a man round
to Winter's house to see if he was there. And he wasn't.
So, just as a precaution, I got the Yard to circulate
his description and a ' stop ' warning to all the ports.

... The hunt'll soon be on all over the country, too.
... Don't worry—we'll get him."

Laurence Winter was actually in a very bad jam at
that moment—a traffic jam. . . . Cursing the stupid
idiot who'd caused it. . . . Wondering if after all he'd
made the right decision. . . . And feeling intolerably
weary after the twelve most gruelling hours of his
life. . . .

He had picked himself up from the ground, half
dazed, as Terry Booth had driven off in the van at
Salfleet. Almost at once, he'd heard the crash. He'd
seen the lights come on in the pub, and people moving
about with torches. Too late to do anything about
Booth now. . . . He'd tried to revive Cole with water
from the creek, but he'd failed. So he'd left him there.
Without any transport, there'd been nothing else he
could do. He'd started to walk away from the lights
and the mounting hubbub. Then he'd come across a
bicycle at the side of the road. He'd picked it up and
ridden off on it, quickly, without bothering about
where he was going. The main thing had been to get
clear. . . .

Once safely away from the spot, he'd stopped and
tried to think things out. It hadn't taken him long to
decide that the game was up. There wasn't a chance
now that he could carry out his plan—and even if
there had been it wouldn't have helped him. The fact
that he and Cole had come secretly to Salfleet in the
middle of the night would be enough. Nothing could
explain that away satisfactorily. Even if Booth had
discovered nothing else at Salfleet, he'd discovered
that. And he'd tell the police. It wasn't likely he'd

been killed in that crash—he hadn't had time to get up much speed. . . . Anyway, Cole would be found and identified. . . . So this was the end. . . .

Winter had had no doubts about his next move. Not at that stage. If he tried to go to ground in England it would only be a matter of time before he was caught. In such a small, well-organised country, men on the run always were. . . . Besides, he had his emergency arrangements ready. Money in the safe— enough to buy an air ticket. Money in a bank account in Geneva. That second passport, that had cost him so much in Tangier, but now looked cheap. . . . Of course, the police would soon be putting out his description—and he couldn't risk making himself look too different from the passport photograph. How long had he got before keen-eyed men started scrutinising travellers with extra care? It depended on so many things—on whether Booth was in a condition to talk, on whether Cole was quickly found and identified, on how long the local police took to establish liaison. . . . Impossible to tell. But probably no more than a few hours. . . .

If only he'd had the cash and his second passport with him—but he'd never expected for a moment that anything like this could happen. . . . So first he'd have to go home. And there'd be no public transport for hours. . . .

He had set off again on the bicycle. At least he had that—and the country was flat. He'd started to cycle towards London. It had been a grim, tiring ride, with a thin drizzle making things worse. He'd considered trying to steal a parked car and had actually looked at a couple on the way, but the ignition keys had been removed. . . . That wouldn't have bothered Cole, he could have managed with a piece of wire, but Winter couldn't. He was out of his depth in this sort of business. Just as he'd been out of his depth with murder. Clever ideas weren't everything. Why the hell hadn't he stuck to his own line? He'd been doing all right. . . . Still, it was too late to think about that now. . . .

He'd pedalled on, weary and sore. Every time he'd passed a policeman he'd known a stab of fear in case he should be stopped and questioned about his business at that hour. But he'd got through without trouble. At Stepney he'd abandoned the bicycle and caught the first Underground train to Victoria. From there he'd travelled by the first available train to Hayward's Heath, a mere thirty minutes by car from his home, where a taxi could be got at any hour. He'd found one by the station, and paid it off a mile from his house. He'd walked the rest. He'd arrived at the house just after half past seven. Now the testing moment had come. If the police had got round to him, there'd be someone at the house. But there hadn't been. All had been quiet. He'd collected his forged passport and the money, thrown a few things into a bag, and been out of the house again in a matter of minutes. He'd driven in the Rover to within a few hundred yards of the garage, parked the car on a grass verge among bushes, walked quickly to the garage, and let himself in. No one had arrived for work yet. He'd found the ignition keys for the second-hand cars that stood in a row outside, cleaned the price off the windscreen of a licensed 1959 Austin, and a few moments later had been away. . . . Two hours, say, to London Airport—and a pretty confusing trail behind him. . . .

It was in Reigate that he'd got in the jam. The traffic had been heavy, but not abnormally so for the morning rush hour. Then a lorry carrying a load of felled trees had got stuck in a bridge arch, and in no time at all the traffic had jammed solid all round. . . .

So here he was—stuck. He waited, in growing desperation, knowing that every passing minute increased his danger. Before very long, someone would be sure to notice that the Austin was missing. Atkins would report it. The police would put two and two together. For all he knew, they might already be looking for it. *Would* it have been better to try and go to ground for a bit, instead of staking all on this hurried flight? Fast in the block of vehicles, he almost thought so. But he hesitated to change his plan now. Where would he go, what would he do?

It was nearly eleven before the jam was freed. Once he was on the move again, he was glad he'd waited. There were no more hold-ups, no more crises. He reached the airport at twelve-thirty. As coolly as he could, he studied the departures. There was a plane leaving for Geneva in an hour. He went to the booking-counter. Yes, he was told, there was a seat. . . . He bought his ticket, giving the name on his forged passport. James Crawford. He went into the waiting-room and found an empty corner and buried his head in a newspaper. . . .

He was back now in a milieu he knew and understood—the world of international travel. He began to feel more hopeful. All he had to do was get past that barrier. Just past the barrier! Then in a couple of hours he'd be in Switzerland. He'd collect his money and fly on. The thing was to keep on the move—to be always a jump ahead of the police. It shouldn't be difficult, with all the red tape, the piles of papers that cluttered every frontier. And he could earn his living as he went—with his friendly face, his charm, his technique. . . . Everywhere in the world there were rich, lonely women. . . .

He rose as the flight call came, grasping his bag, not hurrying, forcing himself to be cool and calm. He knew the dangers. There must be no sweat, no excessive blinking. They always watched for signs like that if they were at all suspicious. . . . He passed through the customs without trouble. Now then—the barrier. This was it! He produced his passport, the passport of James Crawford. He looked at the man who took it from him. It wasn't safe not to. The man looked at him. They *were* scrutinising. . . . This was more than a casual glance. . . . Could it be the faint bruise on his chin that was causing such interest—the bruise where Booth had hit him? Seconds passed—seconds like eternity. . . . No, it was all right. . . . The passport was in his hand again. He was free to go on—free to board the plane. . . . *He'd made it!* . . . Relaxed, now, he stepped out. . . .

" Oh, Mr. Winter . . ."

He turned—and in the fatal moment of doing so he knew that he was finished. A stupid, obvious trick— a check to test the faintest of suspicions—and it had worked. . . .

" May I see your passport again, sir? " the keen-eyed man said.

Inspector Mayo lost no time in ringing Ashe up with the news. Winter, he said, had been charged with the murder of his wife—the fact that he'd been trying to slip out of the country on a forged passport having been taken as final proof of his guilt—but as he'd refused to make any statement whatever, and Cole was still not fit to be interviewed, there was no more information for the time being. Mayo would keep in touch.

The Ashe household was more cheerful that evening than for many a day. Nancy had been almost as shaken by the final, dramatic twist of events as Ashe had been by the first news of Terry's assault, but with her there was less involvement and once the initial shock was over she had started adjusting and reappraising with remarkable outward calm. Sheila was happy, particularly when she learned that she could go and see Terry in hospital next day. Ashe, easy in his mind at last, went off without a grumble when a farmer client called him out quite late.

Nancy had her shoes off and her feet up on the settee when he came in around half past ten.

" Tired? " he asked.

" Absolutely whacked."

He nodded. " It has all been a bit wearing. . . ."

" *Wearing!* A ghastly murder, a running fight with you for a fortnight, shock after shock. . . . That's the first understatement I ever heard you make."

Ashe smiled. " All right—it's been frightful."

" I feel as though I'll never be able to trust anyone again."

" You're not likely to meet anyone like Laurence Winter again."

" I should hope not. . . . I can hardly believe it

even now—that I could have been so mistaken. . . .
Still, there's one consolation."

"What's that?"

"One of us obviously had to be wrong. I'm thankful
it was me."

"That's very noble of you."

"Not really," Nancy said. "You do so hate being
wrong, darling . . . and I honestly don't mind."

Forty-eight hours later, Inspector Mayo called at
the Ashes' home with all the loose ends of the case
neatly tied up. It seemed that John Cole, now on the
way to recovery, had reacted to the charge of murder
very differently from Winter. He'd been bitter about
the way Winter had simply left him lying in the road,
perhaps to die, in order to make his own escape. Faced
with a case he couldn't begin to answer, he'd made a
detailed statement, putting the bulk of the blame on
Winter.

"No doubt he thought it would help him," Mayo
said, "but of course it won't. . . . He's saved us a
great deal of trouble, though. . . . Oh, thank you,
Mrs. Ashe. . . ." He took the cup of coffee Nancy
offered him.

"Right—let's have the story, Inspector," Ashe said.
"It should be good. . . ."

"Well," Mayo began, "Winter and Cole were
old associates. International confidence men. Winter
started out as a playboy—he had quite a bit of inherited money which he ran through quickly. It gave
him a taste for the easy life and when it was gone he
decided to live by his wits. He met Cole during one of
his little coups and they joined forces. Winter was the

senior partner, the clever, educated one. Cole was a kind of N.C.O. They were always on the move, and they spent a good deal of time on liners. . . . They had a rather original trick Cole told me of. Cole would snatch something, a handbag, maybe, from some well-heeled female that Winter had marked down as a likely prospect. . . . After dark, of course, on some quiet deck. . . . Winter would give chase, recover the handbag and courteously return it, saying it had been dropped in flight by the assailant, who'd got away before he could be identified. . . . Naturally, it made an excellent introduction. . . . They worked that one with Mavis Beauchamp, as she then was. Mavis liked Winter—most people did—and she seems to have made a dead set at him. Before the end of the voyage she suggested marriage. Winter talked it over with Cole. Mavis appeared to be an extremely well-to-do widow, and they saw a chance of a clean-up that would put them in Easy Street for a long time, maybe for life. Winter hadn't any doubt he'd be able to get his hands on all Mavis's money once they were married. Cole was all for it, too. Winter arranged to keep in touch with him and share the proceeds. They had long-established techniques of secret communication—outwardly there was nothing to connect them, and hadn't been since their first contact. They were real pros at the game. . . ."

" Fascinating! " Ashe said.

Mayo nodded, and took a sip of coffee. " Well, you were broadly right about what happened next. Mavis turned out to be a great disappointment. She was a proper tartar in her way—close with the money and very domineering. She ran Winter exactly as she wanted to—and as he was dependent on her he couldn't do much about it. She insisted he must have something to occupy him, and bought the garage for him, and the farm. She seems to have had her first husband's business instinct—she liked to see her money working. The only real concession· to Winter's playboy tastes was the boat—and Mavis liked that, too. Pretty soon it became clear to Winter that he wasn't going to get his hands on her capital while she lived—which, as she was very healthy, might be twenty or thirty years. What made things worse was that by now he knew the extent of her wealth—she'd told him, and she'd also told him that she'd willed most of it to him. Sc he got in touch with Cole again, and suggested they should get rid of Mavis. . . . It wasn't really their line of country, but the prize was enormous and Winter thought they could manage it, and Cole was having a thin time on his own. . . ."

Mayo paused for a moment to light his pipe.

" Well, they were clever," he went on, " there's no doubt about that. They thought up the two-pronged attack, and they looked well ahead. Cole insists the main ideas were Winter's, and I don't doubt it. Winter thought of the ex-prisoner angle, and the idea for the alibi came to him when he was watching a neighbour's field being dusted with fertiliser. They built up their front slowly and carefully. Winter secretly set Cole up in the district as a farm contractor—he knew enough about the job to brief him—and by keeping his charges very low and employing a skilled man Cole was soon able to work up a genuine business. Then Booth was taken on, and the stage was set. . . ."

" How absolutely horrible! " Nancy said.

" It's certainly the most cold-blooded bit of organi-
sation I've come across in a long time," Mayo agreed.
" Of course, they took risks. . . . There were little
things that were bound to look wrong—and you
spotted most of them, Mr. Ashe. . . . The unbolted
door, the hiding of the body in the grass, the strangling.
. . . It seems they were aware of them—there wasn't
much Winter missed—but they decided that the
positive evidence against Booth would outweigh them,
and that all that money made the slight risk well worth
taking. . . . Cole, by the way, provided the tool for
breaking open the door, and took it away afterwards
—it was a sharpened crowbar. . . . They used a piece
of sacking to put on the ground before the substitution,
and Cole took that away too and destroyed it. . . .
Both of them wore gloves for the main operation. . . .
They thought of most things—they should have pulled
it off. . . ." Mayo gave a wry smile. " What they
didn't reckon on was an obstinate prison visito—and
an obstinate girl friend. . . ."

" *And* an obstinate suspect," Ashe said.

" Yes, that's true. . . . If Booth had just let things
drop when he was released, that would probably have
been the end of it. . . . Of course, Booth was in a unique
position. He was the only person who *knew* he hadn't
killed Mavis—so when everything fitted him so perfectly as the suspect he hadn't much doubt it was a
frame-up. . . . The very things that made me so sure
he'd done it were the things that, to him, pointed
straight to a plot. I overlooked that aspect. . . . And,
assuming a frame-up, Winter must have appeared
the only person who *could* have framed him. When
Booth learned about the money troubles in the house-

hold from Sheila, that must have clinched it in his mind."

" What was his idea in sending that letter to Winter? —have you asked him? "

" He wanted to frighten him—and there's no doubt he did. He hoped to scare him into doing something rash."

Ashe nodded thoughtfully. " Yes, Winter *was* a bit frightened—I can see that now. . . . When he had me along that night, and showed me the letter, and asked me if it was from Terry, it all seemed quite natural— he put on a most impressive act. . . . But what he was really trying to do, I imagine, was find out how much *I* knew—how much Sheila had told me—how suspicious I was. . . . Assessing me as a danger. . . . That would explain why he was so relieved when I told him we'd taken Sheila in because she was pregnant. His suspicions were allayed. . . ." Ashe paused. " But after that, of course, I went to see Cole."

" Exactly," Mayo said. " You went to see Cole. That was what *really* scared him. Cole naturally reported it at once. . . . You went and asked a lot of questions and you hadn't a convincing reason. Winter never believed for a moment that you wanted your field limed—apparently he'd seen it and thought it was past liming. . . ."

" It is," Ashe said.

" So he realised that you were snooping about, suspicious of Cole, and that you were particularly interested in the lime aspect of the case. . . . In fact, the net was closing in. The alibi was in danger. . . . It was then that Winter and Cole together started to go back over everything they'd done, to make certain that nothing could be brought home to them. .... And, as you did, they thought of lime on the boat. Winter had been extremely careful, that night in the paddock —he'd worn a pair of Cole's gumboots and a plastic mac over his clothes and an old cap, and Cole had taken them all away afterwards. . . . They'd thought the precautions quite adequate at the time. But now that you'd become suspicious they weren't so sure. As you said, the merest trace on the boat would have been enough—and their necks were at stake. So they decided to *make* sure. . . . That's why they were at Salfleet that night."

" I *see* ! "

" Personally, I couldn't understand why Cole had to be there—not until he told me. It seemed to me that all Winter had to do was pay another visit to the boat by himself in the usual way—then, if any lime had been discovered later, its presence could have been innocently explained, because there might still have been some on his clothes. . . . Apparently they considered that, but turned it down. . . . I gather Winter had already told you he'd never go to the boat again—and by the time they'd got around to considering the lime danger, the weather was breaking, which would have made an open visit even harder to explain. . . . And Winter felt he daren't wait for an improvement in the weather, because someone else might go over the boat in the meantime. The threat might be imminent. . . ."

" So what were they going to do? "

" Well, they'd actually thought of scuttling the boat —that shows how worried they were. Loosening a joint in the toilet and letting the water in. But they finally decided on another plan. They were going to tow the cruiser to the mud bank opposite the place where it grounded before, the steep one that Ted Pettit told us about, and let it fall over when the tide went out, and fill. . . . It would have been quite a job, of course—that's why it needed two of them. But it would have looked more natural than scuttling. The idea was to let people think the boat had been cast adrift by young hooligans on the creek. . . ."

"It could have worked," Ashe said.

"Oh, yes, it wasn't a bad idea at all—any traces of lime would have been lost. After that, however great the suspicion, nothing could ever have been proved against them. . . . It's really very ironical. . . ."

"What is?"

"We analysed Booth's handful of dust. We put a vacuum cleaner over the boat and analysed the contents of that, too. . . . There wasn't a trace of lime. Not a speck!"

"Well, I'm damned!"

"It just shows how easy it is to be wrong in this sleuthing business, doesn't it?" Mayo said, with a touch of complacence. "And what a big part luck plays. . . . So actually it was their own guilt that destroyed them. If they'd left things alone they'd have been all right. But I can see how the possibility would nag at them. They *had* to make sure. . . . And then they ran into Booth. . . ."

"Well, well!" Ashe looked quite shaken. "So it was really a very near thing."

"A very near thing," Mayo said grimly, "especially for Booth. Cole naturally denies there was any thought of killing him, but I reckon they'd have had to, once he'd seen them. The two of them there together—it was a deadly connection. They'd probably have found the knotted handkerchief, too, if the rough-house had gone the other way. . . . Still, there it is—everything's turned out all right. . . ."

Mayo got to his feet. " Well, this won't feature as my favourite case, Mr. Ashe, if ever I get around to writing my memoirs—not by a long chalk. But I guess you won't mind looking back on it. . . . You've come out of it well—very well. I congratulate you."

Nancy said, " I think that's very generous of you, Inspector—considering everything."

" Not at all. . . . I'm glad your husband's confidence in young Booth was justified. . . . Mind you, I rather doubt if he'll ever amount to much. . . ."

" It could be that I share your doubt," Ashe said, with a smile. " But that's hardly the point, is it? "

" No, it's not the point," Mayo agreed. " Everyone has a right to his chance. . . . Well, I'll be getting along now. . . ."

Ashe walked with him down the drive. At the gate, Mayo turned. " I reckon you're doing good work with these young fellows, Mr. Ashe—I'm quite a convert. . . . But if you should have another ex-prisoner protégé in mind for a job—try and fix him up in someone else's manor, will you? Good-bye—and good luck ! "

Terry Booth turned up at Springfield that afternoon, having been discharged from the hospital in the morning. With his plastered cuts he looked slightly more battered than before the fight, but not very much. Sheila, pink and proud, spent an hour alone with him in the garden. When Ashe came in from a job at five o'clock they were bringing tea out on a tray, watched with a tolerant smile by Nancy.

Ashe said, " Hi, Terry! "

" Hullo, Mr. Ashe."

" Feeling better? "

Terry nodded. He'd become a bit of a local hero, Ashe knew, with all the publicity there'd been—especially among those who'd most doubted him. But it didn't seem to have gone to his head at all. He was rather subdued.

" I got to thank you," he said. " For what you done. Sticking by me, like. . . . Specially after them names I called you."

" It was a pleasure," Ashe said.

" Beats me how you worked it all out. . . . I reckon I wouldn't ever of got out of the mess on my own."

" Well, you made quite a contribution," Ashe said, with a grin. " After all, it was you who waded into Cole and Winter, not me—and it was you who got bashed ! "

" He looks awful, doesn't he," Sheila said.

" And, of course, Sheila started the ball rolling. . . . Let's call it a successful co-operative effort."

Terry nodded. " I guess so. . . ." He paused, fingering the plaster on his scalp. " Abbott's Garage in Laybridge, they want a mechanic, Mr. Ashe. I see the notice when I come by to-day. . . . So I reckoned I'd go in an' ask for the job. Mr. Abbott, he knew about me—read it all in the papers, see. He said he'd give me a try. I'll be starting day after to-morrow."

" Good," Ashe said.

" Then Sheila and me can get married right away."

" Good," Ashe said.

" Are you going to tell your parents now, Sheila? "
Nancy asked.

A familiar look settled on Sheila's face—a look of obstinacy. " I'll tell them when I'm married," she said.

When Nancy took the children indoors, Ashe drifted in after her. " Well," he said, " that seems to be that, doesn't it? New job, wedding bells, everything. . . . All neat and tidy."

" Yes—quite a triumph, darling."

" I don't know about that, but it's a darned good excuse for a celebration. . . . What about dinner in Laybridge and a nice bottle of wine? Just on our own? "

Nancy looked a bit doubtful. " I'd love to—but do you think it's all right to leave Sheila and Terry? "

" Why ever not? He can't get her into any more trouble ! "

" Don't be silly—I mean is it all right to leave them in charge of the children? "

" Of course it is. Come on, get the kids into bed. . . . We'll be real devils—have a bottle of champagne. . . . We'll go to the Crown—they've always got a good menu. . . . Lobster cocktail, a thick juicy *tournedos* with green salad, and a bit of ripe Stilton——" He broke off. " *Damn!* "

" What's the matter? "

" It's Tuesday—visiting night. I'd completely forgotten."

" Oh, darling—do you really have to go? "

Ashe frowned. " I don't see why I should," he said. " Lot of bloody crooks ! Maybe I'll skip it. . . ."

He went to the window and stood there for a moment, looking out. " Crooks! " he muttered. He lit his pipe and puffed viciously. He looked at his watch. He went into the cloakroom. When he came out he had his hat on.

" We'll celebrate to-morrow," he said. " I guess I'd better go."

THE END